For Andrew

TWIST

MARK L. FOWLER

Best Wishes

Mark Fowler

For Jim Green

ONE

It was a fine day in April when she walked into the offices of Dempsey, Meredith and Twist.

By May she was dead.

I was yawning over contracts when I looked up to see her entering our reception area, and that's when I caught my first glimpse. Wearing a navy trouser suit and her hair done up in an ebony bow, she looked to be in good shape, at least from the back and side. I was speculating on the rest when Angie, our secretarial genius, nodded towards me through the glass, and the woman turned around.

It might not be in keeping with the spirit of the times, but I gasped. I thought of what Edgar Allen Poe said, about nothing in this world being more poetic than a sad and beautiful woman. But then I read too much and I've never tried to deny it.

She was coming through to my office. Statistically it had to be divorce work. At DMT that generally meant surveillance. Do a bit of tailing; take a few snaps, bread and butter and happy days. But then every day was a happy day at Dempsey, Meredith and Twist, as we did what we did, at our pace and in our way; determined not to overreach and not afraid to redirect. Carl Dempsey and Roy Meredith were the best companions that a bookworm dreamer could pray for, and we never wasted a day grieving for the uniforms of two English counties.

Her shadow dimmed the shine on the glass of my office door. I tried to pinpoint the nature of the mission from the expression on her face. Sherlock Holmes would doubtless have brought some imagination to the game, but I was sticking with domestic surveillance. Roy and I usually split those cases. I was hardly up to both eyes, and Roy, the senior partner and founder of the agency, was on the verge of taking a course from Angie on how to paint his nails.

Perhaps it wasn't divorce after all. I pondered the possibilities. It might turn out that she was happily married to an intelligent hunk, with five perfect children and a yacht parked up in Marbella for the rest of the summer.

So why come into a detective agency in Stone? Or *Stone-in-the-Mire* as Carl sometimes referred to it. The town he lovingly called 'the broken-heart of Staffordshire' on account of the high divorce rate. And why come into our humble High Street office, looking like somebody had thrust a needle into all of that beauty that she was carrying around with her, doing their utmost to suck the life out of it?

I placed my copy of Raymond Chandler's *The Big Sleep* into my desk drawer. I was reading too much of the American Hardboiled Detective School and I confess that I was even starting to think in the same voice. It was doing nothing for my identity crisis.

"Mr Twist?"

I held out a hand and smiled.

She didn't return the smile and didn't take my outstretched hand either. I tried not to appear offended.

"Your secretary wanted to take some details, but ..."

She let the sentence run out of steam and I did my chivalrous best to help it past the post. "Yes, she does have an inquisitive disposition," I said. "I really don't know what she thinks she's doing working for a bunch of professional nosey-parkers."

She gave me a look, like she was trying to weigh me up. I hoped that when she'd finished doing so she could perhaps enlighten me too.

Up close put a good ten years on her. If the condition still existed in the ephemeral world of medical science, she had the worst – or should that be *best?* – case of melancholia I'd come across: she was straight out of an old master and belonged in a rich man's attic: oils, Dutch, nothing art school about her; a fantasy creature from another century, another world.

"I hope I haven't caused a problem," she said. "I wanted to speak to you directly, Mr Twist, and privately."

"Of course," I said, pulling out a chair opposite. "Where are my manners? You must excuse me. Please, take a seat."

Through the glass I could see Angie hovering. It was company policy to get details at reception, screening out some of the time wasters. Angie was a dab hand at pointing in the direction of the police station up the road or the solicitors down it, the doctors, the hospital, and once straight to the funeral directors. I winked discreetly to let her know that the company could handle the disruption. After all, I was officially MD, same as the other two.

I checked there was nothing out on my desk that the public at large shouldn't see, and then I sat down to join her.

With nothing but a few inches of desk separating me from my new prospective client, I felt myself pinned back in my chair as though I had been bound by ropes. I tried hard to remember what I had done with my voice, and then I found it but didn't like it.

"So how do you think I can help you, Miss ..?"

It had to be family business, and my money was still on husband trouble. There was a lot of it about, particularly in the spring and summer time. I eyed her wedding ring, waited for her to turn Miss into Mrs, and add a few basics

7

like a name and a reason to be here on such a fine afternoon.

"You're a philosopher, I believe."

I'd been called worse. But still it wasn't how I was used to being described.

"I did once get a book of wise sayings from my gran," I said. "It was one Christmas, as I recall."

Looking mildly puzzled by my lame attempt at humour – and she wouldn't be the first, and likely not the last, either – she said, "You studied philosophy in Leicester."

I blinked. "I didn't catch your name."

Looking into those deep green eyes as far as I could shine a light, I attempted the impossible: to see past the sad beauty, and the way it held the power to knock the common sense and every other kind of sense right out of me.

"Beth Hilary," she said. "*Mrs.*"

I nodded, for no particular reason. "And what would you know about Leicester and philosophy, Mrs Hilary?"

She lightly scratched the back of her hand, the one bearing the diamond. The real itch was doubtless somewhere deeper and I wondered when we would get to it.

"You were a policeman in Leicester."

This was turning into a particularly dull episode from the *This Is Your Life* archives. I decided to get the trivia out of the way.

"You've certainly done your homework, Mrs Hilary: a second class degree in philosophy and a third rate career in uniform. Are you sure you're talking to the right man?"

"I hope so, Mr Twist."

"You can call me Will."

I don't know why I said that. I could feel the effects of it running up my neck and prickling along my hairline into

8

beads of sweat. I tried to redeem myself with what I imagined to be a charming smile. "So you thought you'd pay a visit to the Stone Philosophers?"

She looked blankly at me.

"Mr Meredith took the philosophy option on a Humanities course, and Mr Dempsey had the same book of wise sayings off *his* gran, also for Christmas, I believe. It might be the other way around. The Stone Philosophers, at your service."

My grin dried up. I rubbed at my chest and made a gesture of discomfort. "A touch of indigestion," I said. "So, how can I help you, Mrs Hilary?"

"Beth."

I repeated the name and seemed to make a meal of it. For good measure I threw in another apology and then feigned a brief coughing fit. "What with indigestion and this chest ..."

I couldn't find any meaningful way of finishing the sentence.

"I'm sorry," I said. "It was just a poor joke."

The joke had been poor ten years ago and had since fallen on harder times. Still, I couldn't let it die with dignity. "Philosopher's Stone – Stone Phil ..."

Then the miracle occurred.

She was laughing; she put a hand up to her face as if to contain herself.

"In a decade that's the first time that joke got a laugh."

She was wiping her eyes. "That doesn't surprise me."

The laughter transformed her. After looking out over a wild moor, filled with awe at its dark beauty, I had seen the sun strike the landscape to the sound of angels.

"Isn't philosophy an unusual background for a detective?"

9

It was a reasonable question, but all she was really doing was unwittingly setting up another of my favourite lines. To my shame I couldn't resist.

"Wittgenstein apparently used to love reading detective novels."

The sun had returned behind the dark cloud. I thought she was going to cry.

"So how do you know about Leicester and me?" I asked her, trying to retrieve the sunlight.

"My son was there."

"Not at the same time as me? Unless you were a child bride, and even then – I'm sorry, I don't know what's wrong with me today. Can I get you a drink?"

She shook her head, clearly wanting to get on with it, whatever it was.

"Your son," I said, "he graduated ... another Stone Philosopher?"

Her eyes were misting.

"Are you sure I can't get you -"

"My son is dead."

I heard the ghost of my voice apologising again.

"They found Simon dead in his room."

My desire to stop her there was over-ridden by my inability to move a muscle.

"Simon moved out of his Hall of Residence. He didn't like sharing. It was his final year and they changed his single room into a twin. Simon was a very private young man. He took a room in a student block not far from the campus and a few weeks later his life was over."

She was picking up the pace. I could hear her trying to outrun the bubble coming up into her throat.

"They found Simon the following morning. They said he'd been dead for ten or twelve hours at least. There was a party in the room below and nobody heard anything. My

10

son was up there alone, and when they found him he was still hanging."

I watched the diamond hand lightly dab a tissue around two moist eyes.

"It's okay," I said. "Take your time."

"They said it was suicide."

She paused and I waited, wondering what we were doing; but already I was starting to guess.

I was rehearsing the intricate details of my reincarnation as murder detective when she said, "They didn't know my son."

After a few moments she called off those big eyes and was looking across the room, at the photograph of my daughter. It stands in a silver frame in pride of place in the centre of an empty wall. I count that photo as my one priceless possession.

"You don't think your son took his own life?"

She ignored my question. "Is that your little girl?" she said.

"Yes, that's my daughter."

"Is it a recent photograph? She's a lovely little thing."

"She is. And it was taken last year."

The photograph was taken in the park one glorious Sunday afternoon when I didn't have to return her to her mother until the evening. There's ice-cream covering most of the lower part of her face and she's looking straight out of the frame and laughing. She was five then, coming up for six any day now, and I wish I saw more of her and not just when my eyes are closed.

"Look," I said, "if you think there's anything suspicious about your son's death, you should be talking to the police."

Her eyes shifted focus from my little girl, her gaze creeping across the desk like a shadow heralding a violent storm. Inside my world of make-believe I was looking down the wrong end of a double-barrelled gun when she said, "I want to know what happened to my son. I want to know the truth."

The tears came, and all I could do was get up and ask Angie to make some tea and bring in the sugar bowl.

*

The sweet tea in combination with Angie's sisterhood sympathy did a job of soaking up Beth Hilary's tears, and then I found myself settling down to a long and labyrinthine story. It was a story packed with all the tragedy of the Shakespeare plays that my old school loved to force down the throats of its ungrateful scholars. Her story was a good one, even if it did leave me with more questions than answers, as all the best ones generally do.

As she went on with her tale, a faint bell began to ring in my head.

When she had finished, I waited for a few moments, out of respect, I suppose; giving due reverence to all of the grief that she had imparted, and to allow my head to stop spinning.

Then I asked her, "Your husband died when, exactly?"

"December," she said. "It wasn't the best Christmas."

I remembered. Out on the Buxton road. The Roaches, north of Leek: a man walking high up in the rocks on a dirty wet Sunday afternoon, and falling to his death on the unforgiving road below. The local media had been full of it for a day or two: a grief-stricken widow and a son away at university.

In the space of a few months Beth Hilary had lost everything. I didn't feel like reminding her that bad things had a habit of coming in threes.

But I did feel like making an obvious connection. "Was Simon close to his father?"

"Terence was a workaholic. He never stopped. Simon was the same. They didn't see a lot of each other but when they did they were famous. Simon loved his dad and Terence loved Simon more than anything in the world."

I wondered if that included her.

I said, "I imagine Simon was depressed following the death of his father."

"I know what you're trying to say. But it wasn't like that."

"Wasn't like what, Mrs Hilary? *Beth*."

"Simon missed his dad, of course he did. Terence's death came as an awful shock to him, to both of us. But he wouldn't have taken his own life because of it."

"Was Simon worrying about anything else?"

"He was approaching his finals, so there was pressure on him, naturally. But Simon could cope. He was bright. Studying didn't keep him awake at night. It was a challenge and he thrived on it."

"I'm sure that you know your son better than anybody. But losing his dad, his final exams coming up – maybe it was all too much. It's hard to know exactly what's going on inside somebody else's head."

She'd heard all this before; I could see it in her eyes. She didn't need to hear it again.

Or maybe she did.

Through the glass I watched Carl come into the main office, flirt with Angie, and then head off while Roy, with the heart of St George, played the dutiful colleague, hanging around the office until I could practically hear his stomach screaming through the glass partition, calling out for Mrs Meredith's celebrated home cooking. At one point Roy pressed his face to the glass, giving me every opportunity to take an urgent, bogus call to get me out of there.

But Beth Hilary was telling me again that there was more to her son's death than bereavement and exams, and I didn't have the heart to interrupt her. With a discreet nod I let Roy know there was nothing happening that I couldn't handle.

Relieved of his burden of duty, he was out of the office like a fox after a chicken, all done for the day.

Beth Hilary finished giving me her reasons why I should look into the death of her son, and I gave her my reasons why it made no sense for me or anyone else to waste her time and money.

Then, when we'd both tried and failed to convince each other with words, she opened a small handbag and took out a cheque book and a fancy pen that went with it, writing out an offer that was hard for anyone to refuse, what with all those pretty noughts.

As she handed the cheque across the desk, she looked me in the eye and told me to find out what happened to her son, making her exit before I had time or the presence of mind to argue.

They were hard times in Stone, despite the divorce rate, and the truth was that DMT was sinking slowly but surely into the mythical *Mire*.

TWO

It was another two hours before I finally locked up and made the short drive through the deserted town centre and up the steady climb to Scolders Rise.

The Rise used to be a village, and some might argue that it still is. It has certainly retained the church, the five pubs, the handful of over-priced corner-shops and the quiet, bigoted attitude. I would leave if I could ever pluck up the courage to.

I unlocked the door of my house on Quarry Bank and promptly binned the day's delivery of junk mail that I found faithfully staring up to greet me from the doormat. The fridge reminded me that I had been negligent in my duties over the weekend.

Taking what remained of the Cheddar through to my faithful recliner, I slumped down with a cold beer that I couldn't seem to get along with for some reason.

I switched on the TV and I couldn't seem to get along with that either. The clock on the wall told me it was still too early to go to bed, though I had a mind to rebel against that wisdom. The Box Office crime thrillers and the James Ellroy novels that Carl was intermittently raving about, had recently become standard accompaniments to my ritual liquid supper. And yet that night the thought of such entertainments seemed as tame and unreal to me as the amber water that I was trying to force down my neck.

Carl's hardboiled moods did generally edge towards sex and violence and sometimes that could become infectious with a suggestible type like me. It rarely lasted, though, despite Carl's best intentions to make a man of me. But while we had divorce and police careers in common, Carl Dempsey and I were hardly cut from the same cloth. Whilst I had spent my childhood watching David Carradine getting to grips with Chinese wisdom and fancy Kung Fu moves, Carl had been giving the philosophy a miss and collecting black belts in everything from Kung Fu to Street Fighting for Psychopaths.

Sex and violence would have to wait for another time. I decided on an early night.

"Twist," I said to the mirror, in a moment of epiphany after brushing my teeth, "your teachers were right. You *are* a dreamer living a fairytale constructed out of your undisciplined reading and television habits. But to spite them you'll go far!"

I went to bed and summoned visions of the road that led east out of this fallen Eden. It wasn't Leicester I was calling up, not the real city, at least. I was hovering like a refugee raven over the primary estate of Oldcastle, grown like the tumour it had long threatened to become, obliterating the city and renaming it.

A familiar dream quickly took hold of me, and I was captive to it. It was the one about a philosophy student getting the devil kicked out of him by some nameless thug: a twenty-year-old dream and still going strong.

I woke up sweating like a cornered magistrate, and then I spent the rest of the dark hours thinking about Beth Hilary.

And when it finally came light I was still thinking about her, and wishing that bad things didn't happen to people like her. Losing a husband and then losing a son – how did people go on in the aftermath of something like that?

*

I went into the office early, looking like a dead dog but feeling a sight worse. I needed to chew this one over thoroughly and preferably with my mouth open.

Somebody had to convince me of something.

The feeling of unease was strong and I at least knew the shape of it. It had to do with where exactly I fitted in; and where my name first came into the equation. I couldn't begin to second-guess the wild schemes running around inside of the melancholic head of a grieving widow and mother. I had asked all the obvious questions, but the trouble was that the answers had only made the knots tougher to untangle.

Maybe Beth Hilary wanted a tale to go with the tragic facts. Was that the mission that she was so desperate to send me out on? But in the end it boiled down to this: either take the case or else point her down the road.

I'd spelled out all the reasons for saving her money, though she seemed bent on hiring me regardless, and not the slightest bit mean with the noughts when it came to writing out a cheque. Anything I could find out, she said. *Anything.* And enough money to keep the DMT ship afloat at least for a little while longer, until the tide turned on our fortunes, perhaps.

Was that reason enough to take the case, even against my better instincts?

Leicester was scarcely fifty miles up the road. And I owed Roy and Carl.

When I'd crept back from Leicester, my tail between my legs after breaking up with Carol, and with the Leicestershire constabulary too, Roy and Carl were the ones who had taken me into the fold. Was this my chance to finally repay their kindness? For keeping me on when things had slumped and when a last-in-first-out policy would have been perfectly reasonable?

I shook my head in answer to my own questions. It wasn't just the money. When Beth Hilary put on that look; when she opened up those unearthly eyes, she was a difficult woman to refuse.

I needed somebody outside my head to make a decision.

*

Carl and Roy booked me in for lunch and we retired to the sunless back room where we had the nearest thing to a board meeting since the fiasco over raised rent charges.

Angie brought in the company teapot and a large plate of biscuits to make it look like a proper meeting. She also had a snippet of gossip to share from the daily newspaper.

Apparently a local couple about to get married had won a million on the lottery. She thought that was romantic.

"The divorce lawyer will get most of it," said Carl.

I had to agree. "Arguing how to spend money like that will rip them apart. They haven't a chance."

Angie left us to it, but she took the best two biscuits with her out of spite.

I told Roy and Carl what Beth Hilary had told me. They remembered the business about her husband being killed, falling to his death beneath the Roaches.

"I reckon she pushed him and claimed the insurance," said Carl.

"No," said Roy. "Too obvious."

"Most things are," said Carl. "You don't get away with murder if you try to be too elaborate. She pushed him to his death and her son topped himself – couldn't handle the grief caused by his mother killing his father. That and exam pressure. Case closed. Still, I think you should take the case anyway."

Carl was going through an extremely hardboiled phase again. He was even beginning to twitch his mouth like Humphrey Bogart.

" ... I mean to say, we know what happened and so does Mrs Hilary. But if spending money on a detective makes it easier for her to deal with it, then why not? If we don't benefit from her generosity, somebody else will. You wouldn't see Angie walking the streets now would you?"

When neither I nor Roy looked convinced, Carl reconsidered.

"Okay," he said. "I was joking about the husband. Accidents do happen."

"I don't know," I said.

"What is there not to know? You're overdue a holiday and I hear Leicester is spectacular this time of the year. As a matter of fact, I'm planning on heading over there myself. Remember Madge and Sheila?"

I remembered.

He grinned. "They live close to Victoria Park these days. I'll get the Furlong business done over in Derby and pay a visit. We could meet for a pint."

"Perhaps you can sort this one out while you're at it," I said.

"It isn't me she wants, Will. And anyway, I've got stuff on."

"It sounds like it. I thought Madge and Sheila were married these days."

"It didn't work out. It never does. They need comforting."

"They married the same man?"

"They might as well have done."

Roy cut in. "I'll cover this end."

Carl raised his eyebrows. "Think about your nails, Roy."

Roy shrugged. "We all have to make sacrifices. One thing, though - don't they have investigators in Leicester? It would have made more sense hiring somebody familiar with that area."

"She did," I said. "*Me.*"

"Exactly," said Roy.

His eyebrows twitched, but he controlled the rest of his face with poker style. "Finding a Leicester veteran here, Will - a stroke of luck, wouldn't you say?"

I was thinking about what Roy was saying when Carl cut in:

"Your trouble is that you want it gift-wrapped. A beautiful woman is turning an unlucky life into a mystery and throwing money in your face – and you're looking for a way out? Take it, Will, for all our sakes."

"I don't feel good about taking her money."

Carl laughed and slapped both legs. "Now I've heard it all!"

"He's right, Will," said Roy. "She knows what she's getting. At best she wastes her money, and at worst she buys herself the pain of knowledge. Curiosity kills the cat but it doesn't stop the cat from being curious."

"Spoken like a philosopher," said Carl, making a mason shape out of the fingers of his left hand. "Take a dip into the past and put the lady's mind to rest. Play Sam Spade and have some fun. Let's remind ourselves of the fairy tale, shall we."

His Bogart face was twitching. I sat back and let him indulge.

" ... One day there were three beautiful Hilarys, and then Papa Bear goes belly up and so there were two. Then bright Baby Bear, nine-tenths the way to a University First, struggling with grief and the expectations of a forlorn mother, puts a rope around his neck and does the last dance to an audience of none. How can we sleep at night, Will? Solve it for her, for us, for the world. She's our fairy godmother, so think about it."

I thought about it. But my thinking only confirmed what I knew already. I'd made my decision, made it even before we sat down together. I'd wanted Carl and Roy to come to the same conclusion. But that hadn't happened. That was a pity. That would have been neat and tidy.

"I'm not going," I said. "I'll ring and tell her."

"If that's your decision," said Roy, maintaining a neutral expression as he said it. "If that's your decision, then of course we respect it."

But I could hear the disappointment in his voice and the reflection of it on Carl's face.

*

Carl offered to extend lunch, to discuss the matter further, but I made my excuses. In my office I picked up the phone and fed it the numbers that conjured up the sound of Beth Hilary's recorded voice. I was stuttering through my message when she came on the line.

She sounded relieved to hear from me and I admit I was flattered. The phone was a coward's way of letting anyone down, particularly the likes of Beth Hilary. I agreed to her request that I visit her at her home that evening.

Angie was looking though the glass as I placed the handset back in its cradle. I did my best to smile despite the fact that my heart wasn't in it.

She came through and sat down.

"Do you want to talk about it?" she said.

I looked at her, sitting there, and I thought about how different things might have worked out for me with someone like Angie.

"Let me tell you the story of my life," I said. "It will take about half a minute. You see, there was this guy who once went to Leicester in search of the secrets of the universe. Instead he found a thug to put him in hospital and a career in the police that wasn't all it was cracked up to be. Then he found a woman to nurse all of his wounds but all the time she was conspiring to rip his heart out."

I leaned back in my chair. "What do you think?"

"I think someone's feeling sorry for himself. Why are you telling me this?"

I told her of my dilemma.

"So you're not going to Leicester?"

"I don't think it's right to take advantage of someone, regardless of their bank account."

"I see."

"Do you? You don't look convinced."

"Maybe I'm not," she said.

"What's that supposed to mean?"

"It doesn't matter."

"Angie?"

"What's your real reason?" she said. "What are you afraid of, Will?"

*

When Angie had left for the day I made myself a coffee. I sat nursing it, telling it how fate had brought us two lonely souls together. But the company was dire and my efforts wasted. I tipped the drink away.

I didn't feel like going home and I didn't feel like eating.

What if I did go back to Leicester?

There were a few trivial matters to be straightened out at the office, but nothing pressing if Roy was thinking of getting stuck in again. It might even be good for him to pick up the pace; it had certainly been a while. The money would be a shot in the arm for DMT, and what if I could provide some peace of mind for Beth Hilary?

But if there had been anything suspicious about her son's death, then the police would have found it. DMT could survive – *or not survive* - without stooping to take money from a grieving widow and distraught mother.

All the same, I was restless, and the clock seemed intent on mocking me in slow motion. I put in an hour, and then another, taking files out, putting them back, and in the process making no difference in the world to anything or anybody.

More than once I took out Beth Hilary's cheque and thought about ripping it up, and more than once I thought about ringing to cancel my promised visit.

But I couldn't do it.

That evening I felt even less inclined towards sex and violence, which was perhaps as well.

When I finally left the office, I didn't head back up the climb to Scolders Rise, instead heading west, towards the finer end of town.

To West Hampton and the once happy home of the Hilary family.

THREE

Stone quietly boasts its own Millionaires' Row, located over on the far side of West Hampton, and tucked out of sight like an illegitimate crown. I was not a regular visitor to that part of town. Few of our clients had that kind of money and my own social contacts, such as they were, had never extended into that particular sphere.

I was born in Stone, in Scolders Rise, returning to the area after my marriage and career fell apart. My father was a moderately unsuccessful business man, so I'm told, though I haven't seen him or heard from him since I was a young child. My mother stuck around though, writing weird fairy stories which she would read to me regularly throughout my childhood. My parents split up while I was still sleeping in a cot, my mother feeding me her strange brand of horror stories on a nightly basis.

I was never destined for the straight and narrow.

*

I parked my Civic on the roadside. One look at the imposing driveway to the Hilary mansion had stopped its metal heart prematurely, and I decided to spare it the humiliation of thrashing it, like an exhausted horse, up to the pillared porch way.

The walk up to the house must have taken a full minute, and I spent another couple of minutes ringing on an old brass bell. To be kept waiting didn't seem out of keeping as I stood on that porch. Somehow I didn't mind it.

When the door finally opened Beth Hilary looked pleased to see me, and I went inside.

She was more casually dressed this time, decked out in a striped tracksuit and her hair was hanging loosely down past her shoulders.

The hallway was dominated by a huge canvass decorated with cut-and-paste human bodies, breasts where heads ought to be and testicles where they had no business being at all. The voodoo queen at the top looked to me like a reject from *The Munsters* and the whole thing suggested a surgeon's nightmare in the modern style. *Ugly School* had anybody asked my opinion. But as far as art went, I knew enough to say with confidence that I belonged in the box marked 'Philistine'.

I went through to a lounge the size of my entire downstairs, and while she was busy in the kitchen I looked at the paintings adorning the walls. I started with the sombre oil depicting a dark haired beauty letting the blood from a throat wound leak into a fast flowing river.

Carl would have loved that one. I'm sure he once lent me a paperback with that same picture on the cover. *Devil-worshipping serial killer shedding buckets of blood in the quest for immortality.* I could be mistaken.

Next along the wall was a water-colour with enough full breasts to fill a maternity ward. But all the women were, for some reason, fitted with goat heads.

The oil painting directly above the fireplace revealed a woman on her knees in the middle of a battlefield, her buttocks plastered with hieroglyphics. I hadn't a clue what the mumbo-jumbo scrawled across her rear was telling us, but all the same I couldn't help but be impressed; as was the young stallion standing over her. He was in profile and his appreciation was apparent not merely from the look in his eye. He looked like a Musketeer, though in truth I'd never seen one with his trousers at his ankles.

In that same painting there was a cauldron in the distance and some old crone was boiling up skulls, and the holy man with a crucifix welded to his chest looked to me as though his days were numbered. There were a dozen or so dead women lying scattered and nobody saw fit to wear clothes in that field; and yet it didn't look to me like it was exactly a sunny day. But that's art, I suppose, and I would have been content to leave it at that.

"You like that one?" said Beth Hilary, entering the room with a tray of drinks and nibbles.

"I don't know much about painting," I said, moving away from the sunless field.

"You don't have to," she said, gazing appreciatively in the direction of the eager young man. Then she set the drinks down and walked over to the painting. I wasn't altogether sure whether to sit down, stand up, cough or keep quiet as she put her face right up to the canvas. For a full minute she said nothing. "Terence couldn't see this one," she said at last. "It left him somewhat cold."

I wasn't certain if she was thinking out loud or engaging me in conversation. I almost made a lame joke about naked corpses in a field feeling the cold, but mercifully I hesitated at the last moment.

"He thought the woman was, of course, very beautiful. But he found the young man vulgar. Well drawn, but too superficial in his bearing."

I let another opportunity for cheap humour pass by.

"Terence thought the man rather one-dimensional. Personally, I think my husband might have been a little jealous."

She turned to me and grinned. Then her expression changed, and it seemed to me that I was expected to make a comment.

"I'm afraid that I'm out of my depth," I said. "The woman's impressive, if you like that kind of thing, and the man – he isn't really my type."

"He embarrasses you?"

"Not particularly," I said, too quickly.

"You wouldn't believe – at least, I don't imagine you would believe – how much that picture is worth."

"I wouldn't have a clue."

She told me its estimated value, and I tried to look suitably amazed.

"And yet it hangs openly on the wall of a house that has only modest security. Do you know why that is?"

I didn't. But according to Beth Hilary, it was a simple ruse to fool the common house burglar: a painting hanging openly on a wall appearing less valuable than one carefully hidden away.

I didn't wish to enquire as to why she would avail me of that information. I didn't feel that our professional relationship could yet bear such questions as: are you hoping to set up a burglary, perhaps for reasons of insurance – oh, and by the way, is that why I'm here?

She told me how her late husband had earned his living as an art dealer. It didn't come as too much of a surprise.

"So he didn't acquire the painting for aesthetic reasons?"

"He was a business man was Terence. And he very rarely let his heart rule his head."

I wondered how he might, looking down from the great auction room in the sky, view the wisdom of hanging valuable paintings where the window cleaner could get a good look and decide if it was worth coming back. Did art dealers exist in perpetual states of bluff and double bluff? And was all of this somehow connected to his death – and to Simon's?

"I'll be sorry to see that one go," she said, sitting down and pouring the drinks. "But that's hardly any concern of yours. So, where were we?"

I told her that I wouldn't be taking the case.

Taking the cheque from out of my jacket pocket, I placed it on the table between us.

She looked at it questioningly, and then at me. She asked if I was holding out for more money.

Everything went quiet in that room and I wondered if that was my cue to leave.

Then suddenly she was smiling, and it was a foxy kind of smile.

She got up and gestured me to follow her.

Up the stairs we went, and all the time I was wondering how it was possible to make a wasp-striped tracksuit appear couture. Well, that and maybe one or two less innocent questions.

At the top of the stairs I could see a number of rooms leading off the broad landing. She pointed towards the door at the far end. I knew straight away that it was her dead son's room.

"What you're about to see," she said, "might strike some people as morbid. I hope you can appreciate the value of trying to preserve something of the past."

I tried to tell her that none of this was necessary, but my words fell on deaf ears. She opened the door to Simon's room and ushered me in.

The bedroom was a museum. I couldn't help but conjure up the dead youth as I walked across the wooden floor-boards, catching glimpses of a personality that had passed beyond this world.

I scanned the books of poetry and prose that filled a large bookcase and spilled over onto a dozen shelves, trying to glimpse the significance in the few volumes – metaphysical poets and Latin American novelists - left out on a neat bedroom table and destined never to be put away. A tee-shirt, adorned with a Dali print and logo lay discarded at the foot of the bed, and next to it a pair of pale beach shorts. A handful of photographs of Simon at various ages were dotted around the room, most of them with his father. One, in a black slate frame, looked like a professional job: Simon and his dad in artful black and white, embracing each other, and the laughter appearing natural, almost infectious. They were a handsome pair, and didn't look out of place in a house inhabited by Beth Hilary.

A small rack of CDs over at the far side of the room, beneath a sash bay window revealed eclectic taste, and I noticed a few of my old favourites amongst them. It seemed that the bands that had provided the soundtrack to my formative years were back in fashion among the student fraternity.

A chair with a collared white shirt draped over it made room for a *Now That's What I Call Music* CD incongruously placed on top of a book of John Donne's poetry. There was something sandwiched between the two.

I carefully lifted the CD to find a recording of Jacques Brel's songs sung by Scott Walker hiding beneath it, somehow restoring the room's chaotic logic.

"Will."

Beth Hilary's voice startled me. She was standing in the doorway, pulling me out of one world, back through the portal to rejoin the living. It was to be a brief reunion.

"You need some time and space to do your job," she said. "I'll wait downstairs. There's no hurry. I will only ask that you don't touch anything."

She left me alone with the ghost of her son. But I had seen already all that I needed to see.

*

She was waiting in the kitchen, pouring a bottle of wine into two glasses. I said, "Not for me, I'm driving."

"One glass, surely?" she insisted, handing it to me. I'm no connoisseur, but I knew that I liked it and that I would be sad to finish the glass.

We went through to the lounge where she looked at me expectantly as we took our respective seats. "Anything," she said. "Ask me anything you like."

I emptied the glass prematurely, I couldn't help it. "Your husband -"

"Two weeks before Christmas," she said. "Not a good time to leave your family."

I put my glass down on the small table at the side of my chair.

"It must have been a terrible time for you and Simon."

"Terence was my soul mate. I loved my husband from the moment I set eyes on him. You never get over something like that."

An ambiguity hung in the air for a few moments, and then she told me that her husband had been handling a collection of art works with "occult connections" prior to his death.

Without batting an eyelid she trotted out some theories about his death that belonged strictly in the *Twilight Zone.* I preferred the one about the foolishness of walking in the Roaches during a raging blizzard. Curses and spells were great in fairy tales, and I'd had more than my fair share of exposure to those in my time, courtesy of my family. But I had no intention of conspiring with her grim psychology, and looking for trolls beneath bridges to explain the bad run of luck that she had been having lately.

"How long had your husband been operating as an art dealer?" I asked her.

"Since before I met him. And we go back a long way. He knew the business, and he was good at it. I was born with the silver spoon, but Terence made his own way in the world. He loved his work and he loved me and he loved his son."

I wished I still had a glass in my hand, and she was quick to recognise my need.

"No," I said. "Really, I do have to drive."

"A man of integrity," she said.

I wondered for a moment who she was referring to.

"Look," I said. "I don't want this to sound ..." I cleared my throat, though there was nothing obstructing it. "Clearly Simon had a great father, someone he loved, even adored."

"That's exactly the right word: *adored*. There was a lot about Terence to adore."

"I'm sure there was."

"He would never have done anything to hurt either of us or to put us in danger. But there were monsters hiding in the shadows, all the same."

"What kind of monsters?"

If she meant little green Indians from Venus or Halloween types riding around on broomsticks and collecting the bones of dead children to decorate their toilet seats, then I knew that it really was time that I made my exit.

"Some of the catalogues Terence brought home – that stuff was sick. He hadn't realised what he was dealing with, not at first. I think that people less scrupulous were trying to use him. It was my fault, Will."

"I don't understand."

"I've always loved art, and that appreciation was what brought the two of us together. Then last year Terence heard about an unusual collection and, with my fortieth coming up, he wanted to buy me something special. I'd dropped hints. That's how he first became involved."

"Involved in what?" I asked her. But before she had chance to answer, I said, "Why are you telling me all this?"

"Bear with me," she said. "Terence didn't realise what he was getting into anymore than I did."

"Getting into?"

"The collection was part of a much larger deal. And some of the other stuff wasn't art at all. It was, frankly, pornography parading as art, and some of it was wrapped up with occult paraphernalia too."

I wanted to stop her right there, but she went on regardless of my body language and my half-hearted attempts to bring our meeting to a close.

" ... The people Terence found himself dealing with were not the kind to take no for an answer. He'd blindly stumbled into it – one of his rare mistakes – one of his unusual lapses of judgement - and the door had been closed behind him. There were dangerous people involved."

"I take it that you informed the police about all of this."

"There was nothing actually illegal going on. Terence didn't know how to extricate himself and I didn't want to drum up a scandal that might add to the burden he was already carrying."

"Are you suggesting that your husband's death wasn't an accident?"

"The police, I think, would like to believe that was the case, at least judging by the amount of times they've interviewed me. But, no, Terence's death was an accident, and if they thought I was in anyway unhelpful during their enquiries ... I was trying to protect my son. Wasn't it enough that his father was dead without the police trying to dig something up and the media selling cheap stories and crawling all over my husband's affairs for the amusement of the public? We're not a freak show!"

She took a drink.

"Nobody killed Terence ... but the collection, or at least some of it, was cursed."

I asked her if she was serious about that.

"Well," she said, "more than one person who came into contact with those items didn't live to see the year out. The gossip columns picked up on it and there was always a sub-text: that something shady was going on or else we were just plain weird. I didn't want to feed any of that, for my son's sake – surely you can understand that."

I said, "I'm afraid I'm not following you. Are you saying that your husband's death *was* somehow related to this 'art' work? And if so -"

She sighed, and shook her head. "I'm telling you all this, Will, because I want to get it out of the way. It isn't why you're here."

"So why am I here? The police have already investigated your son's death, and the death of your husband. I'm sorry to have to say this ... but don't you think that you might benefit more from a counsellor than an investigator?"

A look of anger flashed across her face, and then was quickly gone, replaced by a dark determination.

"A counsellor can't help me find out about my son."

I started to stand up and she begged me to sit back down. I looked at my watch as I did so, though I really had nowhere else to be. I tried to say something that I'd probably first come across in a magazine while waiting to have a tooth filled. She held up a hand to stop me.

"Will," she said. "I don't need a psychiatrist to tell me that it's easier for me to believe in monsters than to accept that my only child couldn't live without his dad, and that I was not enough to sustain him through his grief. Not only did Simon have to pull through and still come up with a good degree – my son would not have wanted to settle for anything less - but add to that the hopes of a grieving widow resting on his shoulders ..."

I began to speak but she closed me down. "You've seen his room, the pictures of Terence. He had to do it for his dad, too. He knew how proud his dad would have been. Don't you think I know all that? Do you think I need you to tell me?"

She drained her glass. "I don't doubt any of it. No psychologist or counsellor in the land would conclude differently. Simon couldn't go on under the strain and so he took his own life. It makes so much sense that the forces of law and order find it a ridiculous waste of their precious resources to bother to look any deeper."

"What do you know that you haven't told them?" I said.

She stood up. She seemed about to go somewhere, maybe to top up her glass. Instead she sat back down and looked straight at me. "You decided to take this case, to begin with; before you had a change of heart. Was it the money that intrigued you?"

"Perhaps it was," I said. "I'm ashamed to admit it, but yes. And I'm sorry. If I went back to Leicester, you would be wasting your money. I came here to tell you that."

"But then something changed your mind."

I began to deny it and then stopped. "I shouldn't have let it."

"Haven't I the right, Will, to waste my own money as I see fit? What else do I have to waste it on? It's all I have left."

I started to say something and once again she stopped me.

"No, let me finish," she said. "Yesterday I told you about my son and you listened. I'm not stupid; I saw your concerns, your doubts. Yet despite that I knew you would help me. I knew that I had come to the right place. You must get cranks all the time, people wanting you to enter their ridiculous fantasies to keep them sane. But you don't have the inclination to pacify every nut who walks through your door, do you?"

I looked again at my watch. I had to look somewhere. I stared at it, but couldn't seem to make any sense out of what all the numbers and the hands were trying to tell me.

I heard her voice and I looked up to see her standing over me.

"I haven't told you about Simon's poem," she said.

I watched her walk over to one of the paintings; the one with a devil on roller-skates chasing a naked woman with the head of a blue-bottle through a deserted park. I watched as she moved the water-colour to one side and opened up the wall safe hidden behind it.

She took something out of the safe and brought it over to me.

A photo-copy of a hand-written poem filled a single side of A4.

The poem didn't rhyme and was in verses of four lines each. There were five of them. I wasn't sure I understood the poem, but Simon could certainly write; and along with

35

the elegance there was a strong punch of emotion, though it was all terribly oblique and obscure. I doubted it was the only thing he'd ever written.

"I want to know what happened in Leicester, Will. I want to read everything that Simon wrote. I didn't even know that he wrote poetry, so what else don't I know about my son's life?"

She pushed the cheque back across the table towards me.

"Tell me that at least you will help get back Simon's writings."

She pointed the bottle in the direction of my glass. "Are you sure you won't have another?"

I felt my tongue touch dry lips, and watched as she leaned forward to fill up my glass.

*

The wine was working its magic, lifting some of the tension. We got onto the subject of books, and she asked if I spent all my leisure time reading murder mysteries. I didn't mind her playing games with me; she was good at it.

Her games reminded me of my mother, and how she used to read to me every night. It was only years later that I realised she was sharpening her stories on me, getting them ready for publication.

I made a mental note to get out the collections she left behind and which I hadn't looked at in years.

The talk got back around to the Hilary family. "... Terence's work took him into some dark places. There's evil in the world, evil people."

I'd never doubted it.

"... Simon was a sensitive young man. He picked up on a lot of the stress that Terence was experiencing in those last months. I can see now how much it must have played on his mind. He wouldn't talk about his dad after Terence died. Maybe it came out in his writing - and that's part of why I have to see what else he wrote. What it might reveal. Can you understand that?"

I could understand it.

"I want to have that part of my son back."

"Okay," I said.

"You'll do that for me?"

"I'll try to get his poems back, yes."

"Thank you," she said. "Thank you so much."

We finished our drinks, and we were out in the hallway, when I started to ask the question. She saw it forming on my lips, and I got as far as clearing my throat again in preparation, when she said, "*Why you?*"

"Wouldn't it make more sense to employ somebody in Leicester?"

Her chin tilted upwards, and for a moment I thought she was going to kiss me.

"Let's say that you came highly recommended."

"Recommended – by who?"

"The Professor has been very kind to me, particularly since Simon's death."

My mind was racing, flicking through the possibilities.

"He was supportive when Terence died. He knew what Simon was going through."

There hadn't been a professor in the philosophy department during my time there. Professor Rawlinson had retired early the term before, running away to the Greek islands and taking a Dutch student with him. I saw a photograph of Rawlinson once on the jacket of a book. He had a bald head and big jowls. I wondered what his student looked like and pictured her with long legs and a thirst for knowledge that had little to do with the noble art of philosophy. But I never found out either way.

"I have so many questions, Will. The police weren't interested, and the Professor gave me your name."

"This Professor …?"

"Your old tutor, I believe. Richard - Richard Potts."

I hadn't been in contact with Potts in years. He wrote my academic reference when I applied for a career in the police force. But that was all done by correspondence. I'd had no direct contact with him since graduating. How would he know what I was doing for a living these days, or where I was doing it?

And they made him professor!

He was brilliant enough, though he practically invented the word 'maverick'. But what did I know about the world of academia?

"Professor Potts," I muttered.

Walking back to my car I began to feel the coldness of the evening creeping through the thin layers of my clothing. A fragment of poetry from my youth cut through the years: something about April being the cruellest month.

It was all I could remember. I had no idea how it went on from there.

*

I called in at the office. If I really was going back to Leicester, I needed to finish off a few things and write out some instructions for Roy.

It was late when I wrapped it up, and then I rang Carl. I told him my plans.

"Something about the case pulling at you after all?" he said, his voice ringing with innuendo.

"I'm taking a look, that's all," I said.

"A *look*, eh? At anything in particular?"

"A couple of things to check out. Nothing more than that."

"With every word, Will, you're digging a deeper hole. That's good money to check out a *couple of things*, I'd say. Nice work if you can get it."

I let the schoolboy insinuations run their course. I ended the call, and was about to lock up and head back up the hill to Scolders Rise, when I heard a knock on the outer door. If it was a bum from the Salvation Army Hostel again, asking for a few quid to ring his long lost mother, he was out of luck.

"We're closed," I shouted through the letterbox.

"DI Sykes," came the reply. "Open up."

Sykes looked like a rugby player who had given up stamping on faces for the love of something more brutal. You didn't get looks like that from answering the telephone for a living.

He came into the office, made himself comfortable and told me to sit down.

"What is this?" I asked him.

"I'll ask the questions," he said, stroking his chin with a meaty fist. "Beth Hilary came to this office earlier today and you visited her this evening."

"Are you asking or telling?"

He edged forward and his fingers flexed, now making more of a club than a fist.

We established that his facts were correct, and then he asked the nature of the business between us. I reminded him of the word 'confidentiality' and he reminded me of the expression 'obstructing a police officer in the course of his investigations'.

"She wants her son's poetry back," I said.

"Are you trying to be funny?"

I left that for him to decide.

"How much is she paying you?"

"That's my business."

"I could make it *my* business."

I didn't doubt it. I told him.

"I see. That's a lot of money for some poems."

"I hear he was a very good poet."

Anger didn't improve his looks and his knuckles were starting to whiten. When he asked me what Beth Hilary really wanted I told him she had an idea there was more to her son's death than suicide.

"And you believe that?"

"The police clearly don't."

He reminded me that Beth Hilary's husband had died on a miserable day last December, and that whilst nobody was pointing any fingers, accidental deaths clearly didn't sit comfortably with the DI's world view.

He didn't see fit to extend our cosy little meeting and stood up abruptly. I wasn't too disappointed to see him do so. He told me that, should my investigation into Simon's poetry writing yield anything remotely 'interesting', then I had better be letting the *nice policeman know all about it*.

It was clear that he believed he was delivering a master-class in sarcasm, and I admit that I was close to being impressed. I asked if he had a downer on private detective agencies.

He laughed and let himself out.

I rang Carl back and told him about the visit from Sykes.

"Sounds like there's more to this," said Carl.

"Sykes seems to think so."

"And you still expect to find a few poems and confirm a suicide?"

"That's the extent of it," I said. "But while I'm away, it wouldn't hurt if you could scare up more details on Terence Hilary's death, and anything interesting about his art dealings."

I locked up and finally headed home, only to spend the night dreaming that the Oldcastle estate had become a gigantic beast rising slowly from the bottom of a deep, dark ocean. Its evil had spread though the waters of the earth and was marching on the towns and cities.

The following morning I called in again briefly at the office. Angie made some coffee and I could see that she was fishing for something. When I was ready to leave I paused at the reception desk, but she was busy on a call. I smiled and she reciprocated, mouthing the words "good luck".

Walking out the door I glanced back, and caught her trying to put her smile straight again. But I had seen the changes and I recognised the troubles written large across my face, reflected back at me as clear as a full moon on still water.

FOUR

I sneaked up on the city, but it still saw me coming. I drove past a sign pointing the way to the Oldcastle estate, when what was needed was a pirate symbol warning travellers to stay away from that evil shit hole.

I didn't remember the estate being so close to town: the distortions of memory, perhaps. Or else my dream hadn't been so fanciful after all and Oldcastle really was stretching out its poisonous tentacles, wrapping them around the heart of the city.

Absence had certainly not made my heart grow fonder, and neither had time and circumstance. My fears, if anything had matured; grown stronger with age. I might yet die of fright, I thought, catching myself in the rear-view mirror, and mistaking what I saw for an alien.

I focused on the road, that and avoiding the rear-view mirror and any cracks in the tarmac through which I might fall and so enter an old nightmare.

*

I'd done my homework, checking out the Leicester University Poetry Society website. It informed me that the current president, Stuart Capey, was based at my old hall of residence, Villiers House. As assistant warden of Villiers, they'd even given him a contact number, along, no doubt, with a decent-sized single room as befitting his status as a post graduate literature student. He was going to be around all morning and I'd already established over the phone exactly how I liked my coffee.

I sneaked into Leicester through the southern town of Oadby, its unassuming collection of pubs and shops jangling my nerves. This was the place where the story had started, both for me and for Simon Hilary.

My first year had been spent in the hall of residence just out of the small town centre. Preference was given to first year students, and I had found myself living in a magnificent stately home set in botanical gardens. The same grand old building that later housed Simon Hilary for the largest part of his university life.

I had no difficulty finding the place again, despite having never ventured back during my time in the police.

The gardens were signposted these days, and I pulled up outside Villiers House. I took a moment to steady the ship. I needed to. A few minutes prior the house had been a mere figment; remote, lost in the far away country of the past. But a single right-turn off the featureless highway and *bang,* here I was, and not even dreaming.

I sat in my car for a few minutes, recuperating from the G-force of my sudden arrival, before getting out and walking up the driveway, past the porter's lodge to the extraordinary house.

The place was eerily quiet, strangely subdued, and it took me a second or two for the penny to drop. It was approaching exam time. Party season was officially, if temporarily, on hold.

"Can I help you, mate?"

A boiler-suited beefcake was wearing an air of suspicion. I wondered if the university employed bouncers these days to keep the tourists from disturbing the future of England.

"I used to live here."

"What year was that?"

I told him. He appeared to have vaguely heard of it. "Was that a good year?" he asked.

Strange question I thought. So I decided to reply in kind. "It was the best of times and the worst."

He gave me a peculiar look. "Which room did you have?"

"I don't remember the number. It was on the top floor."

"Attic room?"

"Shared."

"They're all shared now, mate. They converted the last one a few months back."

"Which room was that?"

"End of the top corridor, next to the stairs leading to the attic."

"That would be adjacent to my old room. I don't suppose there's any chance ..?"

He was shaking his head. "Come back when the students have gone. If I'm here I'll give you the tour."

The look on his face suggested that he might want some silver easing across his palm when the time came. I couldn't see that happening.

I told him that I was looking for Stuart Capey and he pointed me in the right direction.

It seemed that even Poetry Society presidents had to share rooms these days, even when they were doubling up as assistant wardens. What was the world coming to?

His room-mate was out, as it happened, and Capey, whatever the merits of his poetry writing, made a passable coffee. He was a frail specimen, but he knew how to hold his head at all the correct angles to indicate the profound sorrow he felt at the untimely end of Simon Hilary. When he wasn't making coffee and inclining his head at the correct angles, he liked to hold hands with himself.

I asked what kind of a person Simon had been, and his measured response came in words individually framed and generally at forty-second intervals. They included the following: private; secluded; introspective; sensitive; elegiac and post modernistic.

A complicated loner seemed about right.

I asked if he had sent Beth Hilary the poem, and he confessed immediately. He had a couple of others in his possession too. Simon had given them to him to read over, but he had passed two of them on to fellow poets and only just received them back. He told me that I could take them with me, and I had the feeling that he was hoping this final transaction would occur sooner rather than later.

Detectives and private investigators seem to have a habit of making people nervous, I find. I try not to take it too personally though.

I looked over the poems, presented to me in a neat folder that I was told I could keep. The poems were once again handwritten, but regarding the content, I wasn't altogether sure what I was looking at. Capey tried to help me out, his sentences lengthening considerably in the process.

"... Simon had, I would have to say, a remarkable facility with words. He would, in my view, have made a very fine poet." He shook his head and suddenly looked forlorn. "It's a tragedy, a truly great loss."

"It's certainly that," I said. "You don't happen to know if he wrote any other stuff?"

He appeared to flinch at the word. Recovering his composure, he said, "Actually, you could do worse than speak to Andy. That's Andrew Lees. Andy's a member of the Poetry Society. Members routinely pass their work to other poets."

I wouldn't have expected that of such a private young man as Simon Hilary.

I asked where I might find this other poet, and the president suggested that I try the university library on the main campus. Then he walked me to my car and said that he hoped that he had been able to help. I assured him that he had been extremely helpful, and then I let him in on a secret.

"These botanical gardens are as good as it's going to get," I told him. "I spent time here and I largely took it for granted. I'm sure that I was not alone in doing so. At nineteen or twenty, you think everything's going to keep on getting better. It doesn't generally, I'm told, though I suppose that for a few lucky ones it might. Are your folks rich?"

He shook his head.

"Then unless they make you Poet Laureate, this is likely to be the best place you'll ever be. Don't waste a second of it."

He didn't know whether to thank me or call a doctor. But in the end he did neither and I left him to his pained indecision.

*

Having put President Capey on the right track I got back in my car. Simon Hilary had moved on from that amazing home-from-home because they had to convert his room to a double and he couldn't take the intrusion into his privacy. He'd have loved it there I had no doubt, appreciating it more than I ever did. He had been my neighbour, in a way – just that he was twenty years late. Or else I'd been early.

I put my car into gear, and floated above a Martian wilderness that might have been a fabrication of a past life that never really existed, except in lurid dreams. The carriageway was waiting to escort me into the heart of the city.

I noted the changes as I fell in and out of lane. I was already within the city limits, the ancient walls, and I felt it. Nothing less than time and its attendants had been tinkering with my past, my formative years, the submerged part of the rock on which I had been built, and upon which I had shaped myself. Yet these outward changes were nothing but footnotes set against the wobbling crest of nostalgia that was beating around inside me, using my cranium for a battleground, seeking elevation and the definitive angle.

I parked up and breathed in the years. What I saw came up to me from the feel of foot pressing on tarmac.

My police days were not the ones that the romantic in me craved. Not the days of squad cars and maps and a hundred attempts at false precision. Leicester, the real and unreal city, could only truly be conjured again by the random tread of an overwhelmed student, who might consider a bus as a last resort, but only when drunk. Student days and nights scurrying around like phantoms from the facades of grim buildings that had frightened me in sobriety.

Were these pubs places I had once believed welcomed me? Town centre watering holes that didn't look much different, somehow; retaining an essence that transcended mere detail; even those with new names and makeovers couldn't fool me.

I was feeling thirsty and I wanted to go sampling. Except this wasn't a holiday. Beth Hilary and her tragic family deserved more than a beer-faced detective getting paid to relive old times off the Hilary estate.

When the business of the day was done, I might find a place to stay, and amble back into town to find out if it really was possible to step into the same river twice.

Or, in my case, three times.

Once you've drunk from the philosopher's cup, you're infected for the rest of your unnatural life. There's no simple path from A to B anymore. That's gone. And who but a philosopher would ever give a damn about that?

Passing the sports fields to my right, I turned into University Lane. The red brick buildings were looking smaller, less imposing with age. But whose age, theirs or mine?

I walked along the lane to the turning into the campus.

The bar was still there, and beneath it, the hall that had once hosted a thousand gigs.

When I returned to that venue on off-duty evenings during my police days, there was no longer access to the bar for the likes of me. My days of privilege had expired. I was a townie on a salary, with what the brochure called 'good prospects'. I would have given a month's pay to go back into that bar, and a gonad to charity to gate-crash the post-gig parties that I'd been too high and mighty to enjoy, on the rare occasions that I hadn't been too aloof to attend. A peasant townie with a pension plan, and resenting students as richly as I had done then, if from a different perspective: Ace-card gone, and with it all credibility; now just a fascist in blue, jealous and afraid, with a career structure to dream about instead of a life.

I found Andrew Lees on the second floor of the library, sweating over an essay on Willie Wordsworth. Lees had clearly had instructions never to talk to strangers, but the mention of Simon Hilary seemed to cause a greater set of anxieties to over-ride him, and the difficulty transformed into one of shutting him up.

He used a lot of words to tell me very little, and I didn't hold out much hope for his chances of making Laureate anytime soon.

As it turned out, neither did he have any of Simon's poetry. He did, however, give me my first break.

According to Andrew Lees, the person that I needed to talk to was most definitely Stephen Harris.

Harris, according to Andrew Lees, was the nearest Simon had to a friend. And Harris was apparently still living in the block where Simon died, the powers that be not seeing fit to close the place down as a mark of respect.

I wondered if Stephen Harris' loyalty to the concrete eyesore had anything to do with grief: his own mark of respect for the friend that he had lost.

Andrew Lees, despite his roundabout way of saying things, was able to give remarkably precise directions when it came to pointing me towards the place where Simon's life had ended.

Not that I needed them.

I stood outside the library wondering what had happened to the years. Had I once spent time here, a teenager on the cusp of life, the world holding its breath ahead of my full arrival into it? Was I ever that philosophy student who was going to change the world?

It was time to let the ghosts rest, and walk the few hundred yards further down the lane to where Simon Hilary terminated his student days at the end of a rope.

I headed off the campus and took the short walk to the blocks.

*

The block Simon Hilary died in was one of six rectangular two-storey constructions. They gave them colours, and his was blue. I spent time in one myself. Yellow. The blocks conjured images of sleeping on floors

49

in post-party style, occasionally getting lucky: a mattress and someone to share it with. Not the worst kind of memories to keep me company in my old age.

The city of Leicester was pock-marked with these cement rectangles, generally containing ten rooms, a kitchen and a couple of bathrooms. Ten of us in each coloured rectangle, all men, or at least with ambitions to be so one day, and nine of them right smelly bastards.

I watched a handful of students come and go, most of them looking far too young to be there. From what Beth Hilary had told me, I could work out the room that had been Simon's.

It seemed that I was in luck. In the window of the adjacent room to his I could see a face looking down at me.

*

Stephen Harris, as it turned out, was an art student. And he had been waiting for me, he just hadn't known it.

He was a bespectacled, studious-looking type, and I imagined his life mapped out all the way to the grave: sort out this little business of a degree, then set about trading the black gown for a red one; next up a doctorate, a turn at setting the academic world alight, a brief interlude for setting up home with a gay lover or a wife; kids in the case of the latter, and maybe even in the case of the former, and then back to kicking academic arse, professorship …

He was hardly into his twenties, but I could picture him, in the long years ahead, converting a diary habit into a set of memoirs in five volumes.

He didn't look impressed to see me, and when I told him my business he looked even less impressed. But he certainly did look nervous.

After doing my best to assure him that I was harmless and that he was not in any trouble, he told me about how he and Simon would share a coffee and talk about poetry and art.

I sensed that Beth Hilary was going to be pleased with my work. After all, Harris had a fair chunk of Simon's poetry with him and he made no attempt to conceal the fact, far from it. And what he hadn't got he assured me he could get.

I was getting the impression that Harris would bend over backwards and even attempt a triple flip with a sideways twist if that was what was expected. I think a lot of that had to do with my careful use of the word 'detective'.

He produced a folder stuffed full of Simon's writing, and placed it on the desk next to my coffee.

Before I set about revealing the extent of my general ignorance in the art of poetry appreciation, I tried to get some dialogue going. But Steven Harris, it must be said, was stiff as cardboard; and so I invested some time taking the tourist route. The trouble with that being that small talk with him was harder work than breaking rocks.

I abandoned my efforts and got down to the business of the day.

"I take it you know about Simon's father dying?"

He nodded.

"What do you know?"

"I don't know much, I'm afraid. Simon never talked about it. I know that it was an accident, that's all."

"Nothing else? Are you sure about that?"

"I'm sure. But ..."

"Yes?"

"Simon ... he changed when his father died."

"Changed in what way?"

"He was a lot quieter. I would say more introspective. I put that down to grief, of course."

"Did he talk about his dad?"

"Not really. He told me what he did for a living, and a little about some of his art dealings. But after he died ... I think the subject was too painful for Simon."

I asked Harris if he knew Professor Potts.

"I met him once. Simon knew him very well."

Harris appeared to want to say something more, but hesitated.

"It's okay, Stephen," I said. "This is a private conversation."

"It's just that ... if Potts recommended a book, Simon had to have it. He quoted him a lot, too. I think he became like a father figure for a while when, you know ..."

"You mean when his dad died?"

"Yes."

"Did you and Simon hang around much? I mean, go out to watch a film together, or go for a drink?"

"Not really. Occasionally we would walk into college."

"What about the poetry?"

"Simon wrote a lot, particularly, I think, after his father died. I thought it was his way of dealing with it. Then one day he showed me some of his writing. He was very good, very talented. He read some of my own work and was kind about it. But I'm no poet, not compared with Simon."

"I'm sure you're being modest, Stephen."

He appeared to be in the early stages of a blush.

"Why do you think Simon took his own life?" I asked him, and waited to hear about grief over the death of a parent and the pressures of the looming finals.

Stephen was looking at me, weighing something up. Then he looked at the folder on the desk.

I took my cue and opened it.

"Would you like to take the poetry with you?" he said.

"Yes, please. But I would like to take a look at it first, while I'm here, if that's okay with you."

He said that it was, and I could feel him watching me as I began reading.

A lot of the stuff was hand-written, though some of it was typed. Some of the typed stuff had hand-written corrections scribbled over it, and there were a fair few arrows and squiggles, all of it adding to the difficulty of getting to the heart of what Simon was saying. He was obscure enough even when he was legible. Yet the odd line would jump out; and if there wasn't a girl hiding somewhere inside those lines then I was most definitely in the wrong line of work.

After a few minutes, with Stephen Harris sitting as quiet as a mouse, I said, "Did Simon have a girlfriend?"

He started colouring up, and this time he was going for the full blush. He even developed the beginnings of a stutter. I told him to take his time.

"It was one night," he said. "It was a couple of months before he died. He was back at college after his father's funeral. He was different. He was quiet, but really intense with it. He went out."

"Where did he go?"

"Into town."

"You didn't go with him?"

"No. He told me about it, later. It was a Friday evening. He didn't come back, not until the following day."

"And this isn't something Simon had made a habit of doing?"

"Simon rarely went out in the evenings."

It transpired that Simon took himself to town that Friday evening, and found a couple of bars, drank a couple of beers, and then went to a club and found himself a girlfriend.

The way Stephen Harris told it, this behaviour from Simon was akin to a cat taking up swimming and then learning how to appreciate a fine cigar.

"He told you about it straight away?"

"He was very quiet when he came back, like he had something on his mind but didn't want to talk about it. It was a while after, quite a few days, I think." Harris thought for a few moments. "It was a poem. It was different to the other stuff he'd written – or at least the stuff he'd shown to me."

"Different in what way?"

"Simon's poetry had always been very abstract, as you can see for yourself. It was like he preferred not to write about anything too clearly, preferring the oblique."

"And this changed after his night on the town?"

"He came into my room and said he wanted to show me something he'd written. It was good, but it was unlike anything he'd shown me before. It was far more personal."

"It was his way of telling you about what happened?"

"I'm not sure. He seemed shocked when I picked up that he might have been writing about a real person. When I suggested it he became defensive. I told him that the poem was good – and it *was* good. It was probably the best poem of his that I read. It was so real. I knew it was important to him."

"And that's when he told you about his night out, and meeting the girl?"

"Yes."

"Did he tell you her name?"

"He told me all about her. He was infatuated."

"Did you tell the police about any of this?"

His face seemed to crumple from within as though imploding from internal pressures too great to bear.

"You didn't mention her to the police?"

"Should I have?"

"Was there anything to tell?"

He didn't seem to have the answer. At last he said, "Simon didn't want his mother to know about her."

"You were sworn to secrecy?"

"I suppose I was. That's how it felt."

I told him that the time for secrets was over. Then I asked him where he was the night Simon died.

It was obvious enough that I wasn't the first person he'd told about being home in Oswestry attending a family funeral. Grandmothers didn't last forever. I didn't doubt for a moment that the police had put themselves to the trouble of checking that much out.

I could see that it wasn't getting any easier for Stephen Harris, and it got harder still when I said it was a pity Simon hadn't given us a few more details about the girl in his poetry. Like her name, where she lived, and where I might find her.

His hands began to tremble, and for a minute he seemed to have lost the power of speech.

I said, "I'm wondering, Stephen, where we go from here."

We pondered that very question together in silence, and then I came up with the solution.

"Why don't you tell me a little bit more," I said, "and then I'll tell you where we go from here?"

Her name was Sharon. She worked in the underwear factory on the Oldcastle estate.

I was feeling sorry for Stephen Harris. Something was frightening him. I didn't for one moment think that it was entirely the fear of failing a few exams.

I asked if there was anything else he thought I ought to know. He looked about ready to cry. I decided to leave it there. It was enough for one day.

I told him that I would probably need to visit him again and soon, and he promised to get the rest of Simon's writing together for me. But I think he understood well enough that there was more I wanted from him than a dead student's poetry.

I picked up the folder and headed back towards the campus. It was time to visit Professor Potts.

FIVE

The ghost of Mrs Greer came stepping along the corridor. Mrs Greer was the secretary who'd ruled the philosophy department the day a nineteen year old William Twist first made it to the top of the paternoster. She peered at me over a pair of triangular, dark rimmed spectacles. "Can I help you?"

"I was hoping to see Professor Potts."

She looked at me quizzically, becoming more solid and less ghost-like as the years quickly receded. "I'm afraid Professor Potts won't be returning today. I could leave him a message. Whom should I say …?"

I felt like a terrorist with a philosophical hang-up, about to leave a garage device behind to blast the department into orbit.

"I was here a long time ago," I said. "I doubt you'll remember. The name's Twist, by the way."

"Like I said, Mr Twist, I could leave a message; otherwise you're welcome to ring to make an appointment. But at this time of year the Professor's diary tends to be extremely busy."

She was no doubt worth her weight in gold, the same as our beloved Angie back at DMT. Standing there, cool and unfazed, the keeper of the professorial diary, saving the man hours that could no doubt be better spent on far more important matters.

I was conceding defeat, when I noticed the sudden change of expression, a grin of recognition stealing over her face. She took off her glasses, as though that might allow her to see me more clearly. Then she placed one arm of the spectacles into her mouth and teased the tip a little. "William Twist! My goodness, yes, now I do remember you. I'm Mrs. Greer."

I let my mouth fall open. "Of course," I said. "How are you?"

We played out the moves until she took the initiative and said that she would leave a message for Professor Potts. He would be back first thing in the morning.

*

I headed into town. It was a mild evening, hardly Mediterranean, but at least it wasn't raining. I sat outside a continental bar in the town-centre, while a waiter brought out a fairly innocuous beer of the low specific gravity type.

Roy's mobile was switched off, and his wife reckoned he'd gone to the local for an hour. She asked if I wanted him to ring back, and I said, "Just tell him that the weather's great in the land of eternal youth."

She assured me that she'd pass my message on. I couldn't for the life of me tell if there was sarcasm in her voice or merely my expectation of it.

Carl picked up straight away. "Solved it, Sherlock?" he said.

"I'm going back to school tomorrow to meet the Professor," I said. "Fancy a beer?"

"Sounds good," he said. "Where are you?"

I told him.

"I'm just down the road. I'm with Madge and Sheila," he said. "How about The Bohemian in an hour?"

I felt like the wind had been knocked out of me.

"Is there a problem?" he asked, when I didn't reply. "They used to serve the best beer in the county."

"The Bohemian's fine," I said.

*

Twist

I walked past the kebab houses, the bus station, skirting the back of the outdoor market and entering into the blackness of town that stretched the few hundred yards ahead of the flyover. Bulldozed buildings that had been second hand clothes shops, record stores and charity book shops, allowed their spirits to mark me as I passed.

And then I saw it.

They bulldozed everything else but left that sewer standing.

I crossed the road and stared at it. *The Bohemian*: the gash in creation where the past and the present mysteriously connected at the edge of the Oldcastle estate. A dozen steps and I could be through the portal, kicking the behind of the king of spooks.

I felt a hand on my shoulder and I swung around.

"Whoa, steady, Will!" said Carl. I saw him eyeing my retreating fists.

"What kept you?" I asked him.

"I had to give Madge and Sheila a good send off. They're going to Malta."

"Hooray for them."

"They've suffered a double divorce and consolidated their gains by moving in together. You have the run of their house for a week if you want it."

"I'm not planning on staying around that long. Did you find out anything about Terence Hilary?"

Carl laughed. "I hardly know where to begin. Let's drink and talk."

*

We walked into The Bohemian like Butch Cassidy and the Sundance Kid. Or at least that's how it was playing on the inside of my head. With every step I wanted to wake up screaming.

The place was deserted. Carl ordered the beers while I selected a seat beyond the bar, over in the far corner.

When he came back with the drinks, I said, "I can't believe you've driven here to drink in this shit hole."

"Who in here's making you uncomfortable, Will?" he asked as he placed the beers down on the greasy table. "I doubt it's the lost-cause behind the bar, and I would be mightily insulted if it turned out to be me."

"Memories," I said. "This pub is why I joined the police."

He took a drink from his pint, screwing his eyes up as he did so and holding his throat, trying for a reaction.

The bartender glanced over.

"Will, relax, for God's sake! You're making *me* jumpy now. It's hardly the Alamo. What in shit's name ever happened *here*?"

I thought about Angie's questions: about my real reasons for not wanting to take the case; for not going back to Leicester, and what I was really afraid of.

I told him what he didn't know. About a second year student staggering from the *French Revolution*: the tomb of the undead further down the road. I'd seen the twinkling lights one cursed evening and walked straight into the arms of the most beautiful girl I'd ever seen.

"In here?"

"Maybe I was in a worse state than I realised. What I didn't grasp was that Billy Boy-Friend, with the tattoos and muscles, was taking it all in."

"Tell me more," said Carl, gulping his drink.

" ... I thought I was in a film. A beautiful girl and *me,* people turning their heads, looking at us - I ought to have known: *What's wrong with this picture?"*

I knew something was coming. I just didn't guess fast enough what shape it was going to take. She with her hands in all the right places and me with my hands in all the wrong ones, and the bar staff treating it all like it was just another moonlit night.

"Dick too hard to see the signs?" asked Carl, finishing his drink.

"Like a caber."

It's amazing it never happened before. The nights I walked around town, pissed, on my own, *student* written across my face. But those lucky escapes got paid for that night.

"Same again?"

Carl looked at his glass. "Not a chance."

I went to the bar.

The man serving was more to be pitied than feared. I got a couple of bottles of lager in exchange for grunts and a few coins. He didn't look a genius, but I reckoned he had us down as snoops the minute we walked in.

I took the drinks back over. "We could move on after these," I said.

"Only after you've got the story out of your system," said Carl "I'm beginning to enjoy myself."

I told him how Billy Boy-Friend took me outside and left me with enough injuries to require an ambulance and four days in hospital, followed by ten more in the student health centre.

"And did you leave him with any memories to take home?"

"Only happy ones."

"And that's why you joined the police?"

"I decided to dedicate my life to fighting scumbags."

Carl smiled painfully. "So where did we go wrong?"

"We didn't read the small print."

"You never found the guy?"

"If I had…"

"*If you had ...?*"

"It doesn't matter."

"I think it does."

"Carl, if I'd found him, I'd have probably run like hell."

"I don't believe that."

"We can't all be like you."

"What's that supposed to mean?"

"You've more black belts than Bruce Lee. I liked the *idea* of finding the bastard, but I never thought it through as far as what I would do in the event. I've avoided confrontation all my life. That's why I was a waste of time as a policeman. Well, one reason."

"We are feeling sorry for ourselves tonight, aren't we?"

"*I* certainly am. I can't speak for you. I was obsessed with finding him, all the same, and I kept returning to Oldcastle. I spent so many nights watching the slugs crawl out of here and back towards their breeding ground ... they don't have so far to crawl these days, the way the estate's growing."

"He's probably long dead, Will, or else doing time. You should forget about him."

"I should forget a lot of things. Like joining the police to nail bastards like that and finding the uniform stuffed with a more qualified variety."

"You're starting to sound like a philosopher again."

"This is the place for it. The joke is that I came back and joined the police so I'd never have to run from myself again. And I've been doing nothing else."

Carl finished his drink and put a hand up to his chin, like he was about to say something profound. "What you've been saying sounds like something I read once. American, I believe."

"That hardly narrows it down. Everything you read's American. In that respect we're two of a kind."

"No," he said. "I can't bring the name of the author to mind. And I can't remember the title, either."

"How did it end?"

He shrugged. "It was such a lousy read I never got around to finishing it."

In spite of myself I was laughing.

A few more customers had drifted in by now and I suggested another drink to show that I was feeling easier about the place. Carl knew what I was up to but chose not to conspire with me. He said he would be forced to provide the barman with a tip, and he thought he'd probably heard a thousand times already the one about how to keep beer.

"So, anyway," I said. "Tell me about Terence Hilary. Was he really in league with the devil?"

"I'd say more likely the pornography trade. Some would argue it's the same thing. But some sick stuff certainly gets passed around in the name of art. From what I've found so far, I'd say Terence Hilary had been around far too long to get caught red-handed with the really nasty stuff. He was playing with some big boys, though, and he was making a lot of money."

"He must have been. I've seen the house. There was some weird art on the walls too."

"You mean porn?"

"Not quite. Beth Hilary seems to have a thing about the occult. She was suggesting that it may have contributed to her husband's death. You know, malediction, that kind of crap."

"Are you serious?"

"She was – at least I think she was."

"That sounds seriously freaky."

"Welcome to my world, Carl."

"I don't know about the occult," he said, "But there's an ongoing investigation into fraud."

"Fraudulent business dealings or art fraud?"

"What's the difference in the end?" said Carl.

"So, fraud and the porno trade?"

"He knew how to protect his good name and reputation, though. It may not amount to anything in the end. Who knows?"

"Did he have any obvious enemies?"

"There are probably too many to count. But his wife was with him when he went over that rock face, so unless the lovely Beth Hilary killed him it was most likely an accident."

I said, "I get the impression that DI Sykes thinks it was more than that."

"Perhaps he thinks she did it. He's keeping an eye on her for some reason, by the look of it. Maybe he's got her down for murdering her son? Maybe she did a two-for-one deal on the family."

I watched as more people came in, a part of me still expecting the thug from twenty years ago to enter the ring and finally call time.

"There's something else," said Carl, tearing me out of my fantasy. "It might just be a coincidence, but it's a good one. Terence Hilary had a business partner – Ralph Sterling."

I knew the name. "Didn't he -"

"That's right. Shot dead in South London. It looked like a gangland shooting – or an execution anyway. As far as I know, they still haven't got anybody for it. Sterling had his finger in a lot of pies. Maybe the police won't look too hard into that one."

"So what's the coincidence?"

Twist

"Here's the thing," said Carl. "Ralph Sterling was shot dead the morning that Simon Hilary died."

*

Out on the roadside The Bohemian sneered at us, a brooding beast biding its time. One day it would change shape and take me down whole. I wondered what it would really take to be free of it – free of that twenty year fear.

The night air was warm and we stood like two idiot gunfighters in the shadows of the Leviathan. Carl looked up the road and took a coin out of his pocket. "Tails we head left, heads we go right; and if the coin goes down the crack we stay the night."

I told him I had a better idea.

We got in his jeep and headed for the university.

*

"It's basically a triangle," I told him, "comprising of town, university, and estate."

"Don't they have one of those down in Bermuda? Triangles, I mean. Planes, ships – everything goes missing, never to be seen or heard of again."

"You're getting the idea," I said.

We went past the campus and I asked him to pull up by the blocks. I pointed to a lighted window on the second floor, and a room in darkness adjacent to it.

"More of that Twist past?" he suggested.

"That's where Simon Hilary died."

I saw in my mind's eye a young man standing on the furniture, a rope around his neck.

"Simon Hilary had a girlfriend," I said.

"Is that still allowed these days?"

"He met a townie. He took himself off one evening and picked up a girl from the local knicker factory. It sounds unlikely enough to be true."

"Unlikely?"

"She doesn't sound his type."

"Anything's your type at that age. Or any age, come to that. Did he see her for long?"

"Long enough."

"Long enough for what?"

"He may have ... confided his troubles to the young lady."

"Does Beth Hilary know about her?"

"I doubt it. I don't think she'd approve. Oldcastle doesn't breed for the likes of a Hilary heir. Then again, as a mother, she might wonder if her son was seeing anybody."

"How did you find out about the girl?"

I told Carl about Stephen Harris.

"Art student, eh? That's interesting."

"You think?"

"In the context, yes. A good cover."

"For what?" I asked.

"What about blackmail?"

"You're reading too many of those books."

"No, Will, hear me out. If he knew about the girl, he could have been blackmailing Simon not to let Mummy know he's seeing a dirty little tramp from the Pants Emporium. Or maybe he knew about Terence Hilary's porn trade and art fraud and whatever else he was getting up to – and he was blackmailing all the Hilarys."

"I don't think so, Carl."

"Why not?"

"He doesn't seem the type."

"They never do."

"I reckon Stephen Harris might have been the best – and maybe the only – friend Simon Hilary had."

"Maybe he was. But if he saw the opportunity to make a lot of money – and if he's bright enough ..."

"I'll bear it in mind," I said.

"So what's new, then?"

"The Head of Philosophy, Professor Richard Potts, recommended a student from twenty years back, and living two counties away, to look into the case. Why?"

"Not two counties away from the Hilary home though, Will."

I looked again at the dark window, and thought about Beth Hilary living alone in the House of Usher, her macabre paintings for company. And I thought about a young man raised in a house like that, and spending the biggest part of his student life in a decaying mansion set in amazing gardens. Then his father dies and home isn't home anymore, and he returns to Leicester to live in a concrete block.

I felt Carl's foot kick against mine. "Time for a nightcap, dreamer?" he said.

*

Madge and Sheila's house was a neat little semi, and it came complete with a fridge full of beer. Carl seemed suspiciously at home in the property but I didn't feel inclined to pry. I wished them well. I hoped they had a good time in Malta. I had no doubt that Carl would be offering all the support he could on their return.

"… Beth Hilary's trying to make something out of nothing," he said, opening another can of beer. "She's trying to make something add up. Her son killed himself, and she needs a reason, an explanation. It doesn't matter how insane the logic, it's better than what she's got. Or she thinks it is. The problem with this case is pulling out. She's going to keep digging until she gets blood, anybody's."

"You sound like you know all about her," I said.

"I know the type, let's say."

"So what do you suggest?"

"What have you got to follow up?"

I took a swig of beer and sighed. "If Terence Hilary was peddling porn, there was scope for blackmail, and the same with fraud. Maybe that's what Beth Hilary's putting me onto. If Simon caught wind of it – or if someone was putting pressure on him ... he would have been in a fragile enough state already."

*

We opened some more bottles, and I told him about when I was in hospital, Professor Potts visiting me.

" ... He brought me some books on philosophy."

"What a swine," said Carl.

"He also arranged the health centre for my convalescence. The man *cared*, I'll give him that much."

"So he should. He had a pastoral duty."

"But he didn't come across as someone just doing his duty."

"And you think you owe him?"

"It's not that. But he took an interest. When he came to the hospital, he asked about my family."

"That would have been a short conversation." Carl held up a hand. "I'm sorry, Will. That's what comes of drinking on an empty brain. I -"

"Don't worry about it. He knew about my mum dying. I could talk to him. And apparently Simon was close to him. Potts would be a good person to have around to talk to."

I drank up. It was time to hit the sack.

Carl was opening up a night cap.

"Did you find out the name of Simon Hilary's girlfriend?" he asked me.

"Sharon," I said. "Sharon McKenzie."

"Any idea where you can find this Sharon McKenzie?"

"Unfortunately … yes."

"I take it," he said, "that you mean Oldcastle?"

SIX

I woke from the weirdest dream. Beth Hilary's gothic art gallery of a home had likely set it off.

I dreamed my mother was writing stories from the grave and reading them to me through the night, every night. The stories were her usual brand: strange, surreal and filled with horror. But there was something else in there too: her stories were mixing biography and prophecy; telling my life before it happened, shaping my actions and determining the decisions and outcomes.

Carl had left a note on the kitchen table, telling me that he was heading over to Derby on business, and that he would try to catch me later. There were two envelopes next to the note, one containing my key to the front door, the other for donations towards a thank you present for Madge and Sheila.

I showered, dressed, helped myself to cereal, and left a small collection of twenties in one envelope, before taking the key out of the other.

It was time to renew my acquaintance with Professor Potts.

*

Mrs Greer smiled, though she hardly put me at my ease. It was the smile of a desk sergeant when you're walking along the corridor for a meeting with the Chief Superintendent and he knows a lot more than he ought to.

"The Professor's expecting you," she said. "He couldn't believe it was so long since you were here as a student. And neither can I."

"Time, Mrs Greer," I said, trying to capture the enigma of the concept.

"The great deceiver?" she said, and smirked, I thought, though I might have been deceived. No amount of chat, inane or profound, was going to talk me out of my blossoming paranoia.

A door opened and out he strode, as short and skinny as I remembered him, and still with a full head of neatly trimmed black hair, his face cleanly shaven. Some things, I concluded, were destined never to change.

A hand that seemed too meaty for the fragile wrist from which it hung was already extended my way.

"William Twist," he said. "How absolutely wonderful to see you. Give me five minutes and I'm all yours."

Around those dark eyes I noticed the unmistakable signs of ageing. He had to be late fifties, at a guess, and not doing badly at that.

He turned to a man following behind him, introducing him to Mrs Greer. I watched the three of them move toward the general office. Then Potts turned and made a five-fingered gesture my way, smiling so warmly that I felt the urge to apologise publicly for my previous misgivings.

In less than a minute he was back, opening his office door, apologising for his lack of manners. He showed me in and told me to make myself comfortable, adding that he wouldn't be more than a "couple of shakes of a donkey's tail."

The room was foreign to me, and at the same time as nostalgic as an old girlfriend's nightdress. The books were a sight to behold; there were hundreds of them: the philosophy of everything.

I could feel a tremble coming on; that old pre-seminar sense of my own incompetence and slothfulness; a reminder of the sweats that accompanied the arrival of

April/May and that final approach road to another summer of examination misery. The day of my final exam I vowed never again to put myself through it, and I'm proud to say that to this day I have kept that promise.

Across the far wall was a miniature library of existentialist thought. Opposite, four rows boasting of nothing but Kant, with three-a-piece for Hume and Descartes and a modest couple for the Greeks and ... what did we have down here? In the far corner: below Hegel, beneath Schopenhauer, his beloved Austrian: Wittgenstein.

I couldn't work out the deeper system that he was operating. Underneath the surface neatness it seemed like so much random chaos.

Below the sacred Austrian, more shelves reached down to the floor. I faintly recognised a couple of Christian mystics and some late medieval thoughts bound up in leather. Some unbridled eclecticism had taken over this part of his personal library, the Upanishads nestling with the Kabbalah and, inter-mingled, some peculiarly-bound volumes that wouldn't have looked out of place in the working laboratory of the full time alchemist.

Down in that remote corner I was further out of my depth than I had been with Kant and Descartes, and that was saying something. I rested my lazy eye back on Wittgenstein and smiled as though to an old friend. Then I gave my final perusal to the considerable section on the existentialists.

I'd once fancied myself as an existentialist. It went extremely well with the music I was listening to back in my late teenage years, when I was happy to put on the gothic uniform and adopt the melancholic stance with that soupcon of attitude. How could you not be recognised as an intellectual – and a damned fashionable one at that – with those trappings? Beth Hilary, had she not discovered wealth and family, might have made a perfect soul mate for that old William Twist.

In my dreams!

I was speculating on how life might have turned out if our paths had crossed earlier in the journey, when the office door opened and Professor Potts was asking if I took sugar in coffee. Shouting my order back up the corridor, he came in and sat in the director's chair at his desk, while I made myself comfortable in one of the armchairs that backed up to a sombre row of filing cabinets.

In the few minutes before the drinks arrived he told me how well I was looking, how thrilled he was to see me again, and, in a conspiratorial whisper, he confided that although he was of course a libertarian who firmly believed in the principles of equality, he was going to have to stretch himself considerably to adapt to the idea of having a forty-seven year old male around the place as a filing clerk. "Oh, well," he said. "We all have our crosses to bear."

The drinks arrived and Mrs Greer grinned at me again before leaving us alone. I wondered if she was remembering my exam results, or relishing the thought of putting a mature male colleague through his secretarial paces. The world could be a perverse place at times.

He asked how life had been treating me and I furnished him with the basics. It struck me, as I was talking, how I had the knack of making my entire life seem to be one long compromise. I suggested that perhaps philosophy hadn't been the right choice of subject at all for such a shallow thinker.

"I disagree. I think you chose wisely," he said. "You could have done well, had you come here to find out about philosophy."

I must have frowned.

"It would amaze you," he said, "how few students arrive with any real sense of academic curiosity. Eighteen, nineteen – it's too young, in most cases. Curiosity lies elsewhere at that age."

"Was that true for Simon Hilary?" I asked him.

"Simon was an exception, in my experience. He was intelligent enough, though he was hardly a genius. What marked him out was his application. He was incapable of distraction. Simon was here because he had a thirst for knowledge – and I mean knowledge of the academic kind. His curiosity was satisfied in the library and back at the little desk in his room. At least, that's how it was until his father died."

I noted his reference to the 'little desk in his room'.

"Did you visit Simon?" I asked.

"I did. I knew that he was unhappy about the change to his accommodation, and so I dropped by one afternoon to take him a moving in present."

"That was kind of you," I said.

"One does one's best."

"Did you take him a philosophy book, by any chance?"

"I'm nothing if not predictable!"

"You noticed a change in Simon – after his father died?"

"It was hardly subtle."

And neither was I. "Why do you think he took his own life?"

It was like asking a politician a direct question on how he intends making the world a better place; or asking a philosopher about the meaning of life.

Instead of answering me, Potts delivered a lecture, and a wide-ranging one, as it turned out. He took in theories of personal identity, the spiritual bankruptcy of twenty-first century western culture; he quoted Leibniz, Rousseau and

Pascal, and I hadn't the first clue what he was talking about.

I let him ramble on, admiring a man at his work. I'd admired him a long time ago and once thought him the cleverest man alive. But now I could see that his greatest talent was for bull-shitting. I could tell that one of us had changed over the years, and I was doubting that it was him.

After he'd had a play with my time and patience I brought him back to the matter at hand.

"You think that his father's death caused the changes in Simon? That was the reason for his suicide?"

He smiled. "You must have gathered by now that it was *I* who brought you into this."

"Mrs Hilary said that you recommended me, yes."

"Which no doubt perplexes you."

"Well…"

"Tell me, why do *you* think I wanted you to help?"

"I'd prefer it if you just told me your reasons."

He shook a finger at me. "Assemble the evidence. Let's see what it adds up to."

I played the game. "I knew this area as a policeman. You wrote me a reference when I applied to join the force, and you probably have some links with them."

"Go on," he said.

"You could have easily found out that I was back in Staffordshire, and based not that far from Mrs Hilary. Colleagues on the force here would know that I was doing some private investigating these days. Simon Hilary and I both came to this university and we both studied philosophy. That's it, that's all I've got. How did I do?"

The way he continued looking at me made me wonder for a moment if I was still talking. At last he said, "Very succinct. Not often a quality found amongst philosophers, I'm ashamed to say."

He wasn't kidding.

"But then I was never a great philosopher," I said.

"Like I suggested, you were here on a different mission. I think you wanted your philosophy served up with a storyline and a strong flavour of aphorism. I recall a fondness for Nietzsche; I don't recall a fondness for the linguistic schools."

At least he hadn't mentioned David Carradine and the Kung-Fu school.

Not wishing to tempt him, I got the subject back to the Hilary family. But if I was hoping that easy answers were waiting - and I most certainly was - then disappointment was on its way round again.

"You must have formed a lot of useful contacts in the local area, through your career in the police," he said. "Useful, I mean, to your present occupation. I imagine that doing what you do back in Staffordshire must be a little like beginning all over again."

I hadn't looked at it that way. But he was right. Leicester seemed a lot of baggage; building up contacts and local knowledge that was of little use to me two counties away. I was a detective doing routine work, though, and not some high-flyer trying to make the big time. I had found two colleagues with the same outlook and the same lack of ambition, and I had no wish to move into a bigger league here, there or anywhere else.

"I can see that you have a question," he said.

"I have two," I said. "Why exactly did you recommend me; and do you have any reason to think Simon did not take his own life?"

He thought for a moment. "Let me put your second question a slightly different way. Do you think Mrs Hilary has any cause to think that her son did not commit suicide?"

I was starting to get a little tired of his style, yet still I took a moment to get my head around what was going on beyond the obvious distinction; the possible shades of meaning.

"She's still in a state of grief," I said. "I'm not sure she's come to terms ... that she's fully rational about her son's death. That's hardly surprising, is it? If she has information, or concrete, specific suspicions, she needs to detail them and take them back to the police. Otherwise, I'm afraid there's nothing else -"

"Do you have any lines of enquiry to follow up?"

"If there was anybody close to Simon at the time of his death, I would like to speak to them, naturally. But my understanding is that he was something of a loner."

I watched Potts carefully.

Did he know about Sharon McKenzie? Would he tell me if he did?

After thoroughly checking that none of his finger-nails needed trimming, he said, "Simon came here to study philosophy, the same as I did, once upon a time. He, like me, came across an account of the life of Wittgenstein that fired something up inside."

He looked at me as though checking that I registered the name. I felt honour bound to satisfy his curiosity in the matter. I said, "I remember trying to read the *Tractatus,* but all I understood was the closing line, about what you can't speak of being better left to the silence."

He laughed. "I remember you using that quotation as a short cut; an excuse for not writing an essay on Logical Positivism. The essence of your 'argument' was that logical positivism was something that should be passed over in silence. I admired your arrogance but, unfortunately for you, I put more store by your apparent laziness. You see, I once tried the same thing myself, except that I got away with it. My tutor had clearly never imagined a philosophy student to be capable of such a flaw in character.

"But we digress. Simon, like myself, and like Wittgenstein too, for that matter, liked to stay on the outside. Not a party animal or part of any recognisable group; yet still needing human company. Not a misanthropist on any level, you understand."

"Did Simon have any friends or make any enemies that you know of?"

Potts spiralled off again, with a discourse on the meaning of friendship and what he called 'the elusive dichotomy that distinguished a friend from an enemy.' He made it sound like the key to understanding everything. But it was all professional parlour games.

"So you're not aware of anyone significant?"

No girlfriend from the Oldcastle Knicker Factory?

His phone was ringing. He answered it, and then looked at his watch. "I'll be along in five minutes."

I asked if he had read any of Simon's poetry.

"Unfortunately not," he said. "I'm aware that Mrs Hilary would love to get her son's writing back, understandably. I didn't actually know that Simon had written poetry until she mentioned it. But then I think that any mystery, the more you dig down, is guaranteed to reveal a treasury of surprises. That must be what makes your job so fascinating. After all, even Wittgenstein was an avid fan of the detective story – did you know that?"

I couldn't deny it.

"He believed he'd said it all, but you never can say it all. There's always something you've missed; another layer to travel through. He came back to philosophy, formed another, entirely different school of thought from the one he had initiated with the *Tractatus*. Two completely different, totally original schools of philosophy – and in a single lifetime."

He started laughing. I was tempted to take the easy way and just go with it. Yet the coward in me knew that he would hardly be fooled. I gave the famous Twist blank look and its coinage was recognised and accepted graciously.

"Excuse my foolish sense of the absurd," he said. "Of course, had he lived two lifetimes, it would not have seemed so remarkable at all. But sometimes, when we think our picture of the world is the only possible one, something happens and we have to tear up that picture and replace it."

He stood up, signalling that my time was up.

But I hadn't finished and I remained sitting down.

"Do you have any reason to believe that Simon did not take his own life?"

"You've already asked me that."

"And I'm still waiting for your answer."

"Mrs Hilary," he said, "has a right to know. That is ... if there is anything *to* know. Maybe there isn't. Or maybe there is but we are not able to locate the nature of it. Looking at my bookshelves I'm sure that you must have deduced by now that I have become rather interested in existentialism."

"I've noticed," I said.

"I used to think that existentialism was merely a fashionable conceit, a movement made out of incomprehensible writings by pseudo-philosophers like Kierkegaard, Nietzsche and so on. Fertile ground for artists of all persuasions, not least musicians and novelists, and yet hardly fruitful material for the serious student of philosophy itself."

He sat back down in the armchair. "Lately, I confess, I have grown up and out of some quite destructive conceits of my own. I'm more suspicious these days of absolute truths, in whatever guise they might come. We all like a tidy ending, Wittgenstein included, though he at least suggested that greater truths were out there, despite the fact that we might not have the facility to attain those types of truth. He loved a murder mystery, we are told. And so do I."

"I'm not sure I follow."

"Coming here today, Will. Excuse me for saying this; excuse me for using your valuable time to talk like some eccentric old fool too long at school. But for what it's worth: there are no mere accidents. Your life, Simon Hilary's life, my life – *threads* that cross in places and reveal *patterns in the cloth*. Your job brought you here, but you are also on what might be termed *an existential voyage*, a discovery of sorts. It may turn out to be more mysterious than any murder mystery. But then again ... it might not."

I glanced at his collection of exotically bound esoteric volumes, and wondered how far he had conspired, fuelling Beth Hilary's determination to believe in a world of make believe. I made a hash of raising the point and he quickly beat me back down once again, this time with a brief lecture on the dark world of grief psychology.

At last he stood up. "Enough for today, I think. I recommended you, Will, because you are the best man for the job. But you can only do your best. Good luck."

With that he held out his hand. "And if those poems exist," he said, "then I sincerely hope they bring Mrs Hilary some comfort. It's impossible to know for sure what goes on in the mind of a young man. I'm sure you would agree about that at least."

*

He hadn't changed; still playing games for a living, and as a hobby too; filling me with the promise of mighty revelations, and delivering precisely nothing. He had recommended me, and yet he refused to say why.

He was in the habit of creating enigmas, conjuring them out of the thin air, and making mundane existence an exciting place for dreamers.

Fair dues. But there was more to it.

I was being used. I just couldn't work out the angle.

SEVEN

All those years on the police force, and I never came to terms with Oldcastle. I couldn't hear 'Leicester' or see the road signs, without conjuring up a vision of that estate; the tumour taking over the city.

Every town has its secrets, its tragedies; Stone, too, once you started turning over the rocks. But they are human secrets, flesh and blood stories that tell of the weakness, the frailties, the deadly sins that come as part and parcel of the heritage of Adam's sons and daughters.

But when the wise city fathers built a living graveyard from the remains of an ancient fortress, and called it Oldcastle ...

*

I found a familiar café on the outer rim of the estate, and called in. I'd used the place in my time on the force, though not very often.

It was close to a row of shops: a video store, a launderette, a small post office, and a pie shop. There were rarely more than half a dozen people in the cafe at any one time, and it was hard to see how they kept the business going. The sausage sandwich was good, though, and the coffee was strong.

I watched the comings and goings; the women calling in while their washing spun around next door, people drifting in with cashed giros from the post office, and splashing out on the soup of the day. The place had a rhythm: half a dozen in, half a dozen out.

Possibly I had misjudged it. You were never likely to get killed in the rush, but business seemed steady nevertheless. I wondered if my time away from Oldcastle had made my impression of the place more than a little redundant. Perhaps I needed to see it with the eyes of the present, and not the past. But that's always easier in books than in life itself.

Before leaving I asked for directions to *Custers Underwear Emporium*. Paranoia was sweeping over me again. I imagined redneck voices telling me that I didn't want to go there. That it wasn't a place for strangers. Fear spreading from face to face as my question was passed from one staff member to the next, then to one of the tables, then another, as eyes narrowed and voices lowered.

Nobody seemed to have heard of *Custers*. Was I certain that was the name?

There was a lot of laughter and strange looks. Was I certain someone wasn't having a laugh at my expense?

The question as to where this place might be spread to everyone in the café, and as customers came in they were invited to join in the mystery. Then a woman with a head scarf suddenly erupted. "He means *Carters*! It's on Shit Road!"

The old proprietor translated. *Carters,* the underwear factory, was located on the Industrial Estate a couple of miles away. I asked how to find the place, and he went back to the woman with the scarf, who for some reason preferred not to communicate with me directly, but rather through her translator, who happened to speak the same language.

A couple of other customers joined in with the directions, as they did their collective best to establish the easiest route for an outsider to follow. Real community spirit in action: heads together, trying to help, problem solving, showing welcome and warmth to a stranger. They told me all I needed to know. No wild looks or nods and winks and shakes of the head. No 'you don't want to go up there, boy' redneck grunts. They didn't even advise grenades and rocket launchers.

Maybe things really had changed in Oldcastle.

*

The industrial estate was on the far north-east side of the vast estate. There was no major artery leading to it, and the map they had drawn for me, on a café napkin, had more twists and turns than the average plot in a mystery thriller. The road indicated didn't appear to exist, and I began to wonder if the cafe community had really been so helpful after all.

Appearing to have over-shot the road I was looking for, I stopped the car. A man was walking towards me. Attached to a length of chain was a dog every bit as ugly as its owner.

I looked back at my map, and waited for him to pass by my car. But his dog kept stopping; a piss and a sniff, a sniff and a piss. Then it was against the side of my car, sniffing at the wheels while its owner stood and glared at me. I wondered if one of them at least was thinking of taking a shit by the side of the road.

I felt like a policeman again, exposed and vulnerable in this place. The student minding his own business all those years ago, and singled out and set up for the vicious attack from which he was never to recover.

They were still standing there, the handsome couple. I couldn't see what the dog was doing, and neither could its owner, who was more intent on watching what I was doing.

What the hell, I thought, and pressed the button on the console. The passenger window slid down.

"Excuse me, mate. Do you happen to know -"

But I never got the chance to finish my sentence. I never managed to clarify the situation, to comfort him in the knowledge that I wanted to know where a road was, and not to in any way challenge him for what his dog might be doing against the wheel of my car.

"If you don't like it," the man growled, "then fuck off!"

A loud bark issued, and the dog's face appeared through the passenger window, teeth bared above two sharply clawed paws.

Those were my only directions, and I took them. I sped off, my re-assessment underway, and that old *deja vu* as strong as the smell of vomit. I headed down the street until I could no longer see the man or his dog in my rear view.

A hundred yards on and a woman was walking towards me. My window was still down. I slowed, watched her looking at my car, taking in its unfamiliarity, and eyeballing me through the windshield. I pulled to a halt.

As she walked past my car, she ducked her head towards the open window, and without slowing her pace, yelled, "Fuck off!" at me with such vehemence that I was sure it must have reached the ears of the man and his dog, and that even now they would be charging cavalry style to aid and abet this vulnerable maiden who was being accosted by some sick stranger-pervert in his Jap-loving Honda.

I drove on, wondering how in the name of reason I could ever seriously put Simon Hilary here, no matter how smitten by the unfamiliar scent of his underwear girl.

I covered just about every road in that corner of Oldcastle. I was starting to feel like I was trapped inside a video game, in which I had to turn corners and avoid meeting any of the exterminating angels that teemed around, and who would destroy me on sight.

It was by accident, in the end, when I turned a random corner and found the entrance to the estate. I looked again at the map, and suddenly it did make sense. Everything but the name of the road that I had been looking for. Collingwood Lane was better known around there as Johnson's Wood. I gave them the benefit of the doubt.

I drove another mile past broken shacks housing dozens of businesses, dumping grounds and a car graveyard that might on reflection have been a car park. No sign of the long-gone wood.

I was looking for *Carters,* expecting to see a Dickensian workhouse with scenes straight out of *Oliver*. But *Carters* turned out to be nothing so grand. A pre-fab with windows too dirty to see through and a reception area as inviting as an execution yard.

I pulled to a halt and got out. Immediately two security men came out of the front of the building, heading for me at speed, like a couple of guided missiles with dynamite for brains.

"You can't park here, mate! You need a permit or we'll clamp you."

I appreciated the warning. How kind of them.

"Is there anywhere around here I can park?"

One of them pointed with a fat and bleeding thumb. "Around the back, mate! But if you go into the reserved spaces we'll clamp you."

They were clearly itching to get some clamping done. I toyed with the idea of giving them some advice: don't warn in future, just do it. Earn yourselves a nice bonus. They needed a break, and a life to go with it.

I drove around the back and found a space as big as a football field, and with no reserved spaces anywhere near. I wondered if they would clamp me anyway.

There was no customer entrance at the back, and so I walked around to reception. A dusty looking woman who might have had a glint in her eyes half a century ago, asked if she could help. I said I needed to speak to one of the employees.

"What department?"

"Underwear."

She gave me a look down a long and pointed nose.

"What name?"

"Twist."

"We don't have anybody here with that name."

"Sharon, then."

That look again.

"We have a number of girls with the name *Sharon*."

"MacKenzie."

She checked a chart. "Due on her break. You can take a seat if you want."

I looked behind me. There was a two-seater couch with the springs sticking out of the sides. "I don't mind standing," I said.

"Mr Twist, you say? Can I ask what your business is?"

"Yes, of course. I'd like to see Sharon."

She walked away, muttering under her breath, and disappeared through a door marked 'Staff Only'. A minute later she was back at her post, and a few minutes after that a young woman with shoulder length blond hair appeared in reception.

"You this Twist?"

"Sharon MacKenzie?"

"What do you want? Who are you?"

I asked if we could talk in private.

"I'm at work." She glanced at the older woman behind her, who was taking it all in. "What's it about?"

"I'd rather we talked in private."

87

The older woman said, "I can call security if he's bothering you."

But Sharon McKenzie was curious. "I can handle it," she said, looking at me. "We'll go outside. You've got two minutes, max."

*

We stood out at the front of the building. "Okay," she said. "What is it?"

I told her. Surprise flickered for an instant; she contained it.

"What do you want to know about *him* for? Who are you?"

I told her who I was and what I wanted.

"He killed himself. What else is there to say? I knocked around with him a few times and that was it. There's nothing more to it. Who told you about me?"

"That doesn't matter."

"Well maybe it matters to me! If some fucker's pointing the finger, I want to know. Why do you keep looking at my hair?"

"Are you a natural blond?"

A split-second of humour moistened her lips but in a flash it was gone. Her eyes turned icy. "Are you some fucking pervert?"

"I was expecting long and dark for some reason."

"Are you the hair police? Someone give a description, did they? What's all this about? Simon's dead and I've moved on. I did nothing wrong, unless they've made shagging students illegal for townies now."

When she raised it, her voice had the quality of razor blades cutting into glass.

"We could go somewhere else to have this conversation, if you would prefer," I said.

"You mean the police station?"

I left her to answer that, and she did so, the aggression disappearing from her voice. Whatever else this girl was, she was more than a one-trick pony. Her voice had become soft, almost seductive. I wondered how many parts she could play.

She started to talk, and she certainly knew how to. As though cramming the whole Simon Hilary affair into a five-minute factory break had become an Olympic sport, and she had herself down for the gold medal. She was a class act, was Sharon McKenzie; making a lot of sound but telling me next to nothing.

I told her so and watched her eyes blaze. She was at the crossroads: about to end the conversation or throw me some titbits.

I saw the decision sweep across her face. Maybe it was an aversion to police stations that did it.

She told me how Simon had met her in town and how she had taken him back to the house that she shared with her mother and step father. They had seen each other, off and on, for a few weeks.

"He did something weird like philosophy or some shit like that."

"You knew Simon had recently been bereaved?"

"You mean like his old man dying? He told me about it. Was like my father died, you know, my real father, not *Cartwright*."

She practically spat the name out.

I was intrigued. "Cartwright?"

She was suddenly nervous, as though regretting bringing up the name.

I pressed her. "Who's Cartwright?"

Again she brought her emotions quickly under control. "Just my step-dad," she said, like it was no big deal at all. Then: "But what I mean is, like, it was something we had in common, me and Simon. All we had in common, really."

"How do you mean?"

"Obvious, isn't it? Him at the Uni, me at the factory: hardly the perfect couple, were we? But we had that in common, losing your dad, you know, and we got on alright. He wasn't a snob or anything. Nicest bloke I ever met, tell you the truth. He didn't know much when I first met him, though."

She grinned, her eyes flaming with mischief. "You know what I mean? He was all innocent. But I'm a good teacher. I'm generous like that." She looked at her watch. "Anyway, I've got to be going or they'll make me work over or dock me."

"What time do you finish?"

"Are you after a date or something?"

She was looking at me intently, her eyes changing tone and colour with every passing second. Weighing me up; the situation, the possibilities, the dangers.

There was something formidable about Sharon Mackenzie, and I could see that she was wasted at *Carters*.

At last she said, "Don't see why not. I mean, if you was to take me out for some drinks or something, then I might be able to tell you some more."

"About what?"

"About whatever you want to know."

I watched her go. Then I went to see if my car had been clamped.

EIGHT

They were bringing the clamps as I drove off. I thanked them through my car window. They didn't seem to know what I was talking about, and I didn't stop to explain.

I drove back to the student blocks, not expecting Stephen Harris would have had chance to get the rest of Simon's poetry. I imagined him head down all the way to the finals.

But there was something I wanted to talk to him about.

*

I can't say that he looked thrilled to see me. But then a conscientious student like Stephen was never going to be welcoming of distractions.

"Sharon seems like a nice girl," I said, as we walked up to his room.

He looked a little stunned.

"You've been to see her?" he asked.

I told him how she'd changed her appearance a little, that long dark hair replaced by a more natural blond. He blushed and I wondered what good a university education was doing him.

He made me a coffee, and by the time he'd handed it to me his face had cooled back to its natural sun-starved pasty white. I thanked him for the drink and said, "I can see why Simon wrote poems about her. I'd say he was a bit of a dark horse to land somebody like her."

Harris was clearly uncomfortable with the conversation, but I still wasn't certain exactly why.

"You didn't like her?" I said.

"I didn't know her."

"But she was not your type?"

"Hardly," he said. "No, I don't mean …"

"Don't mean what, Stephen? That she's about thirty steps down the social ladder? Did you not approve of Simon's relationship with her?"

He was stuck for words and I was in no hurry. I could wait – though he never did find the words to answer my question. Instead, he found some more of Simon's poetry and showed it to me. It looked to me like he was banking on thrusting it into my grubby, working class hands and closing the door behind me for the last time.

There were three folders with about as many poems in each of them.

"How come you didn't have all this the last time I visited?" I asked him.

"A friend of mine was looking over them," he said, and not very convincingly.

It crossed my suspicious mind that he already had these poems in his possession, but had wanted to check them over before handing them to me. Maybe he'd been through them, and taken out stuff that I was not to see, for whatever reason.

I said, "Into poetry, is he, this friend of yours?"

He was colouring up again. In that moment I could see that he was incapable of lying significantly about anything.

"What you mean, Stephen, is that the poetry was in safe keeping."

He nodded. "I didn't want the police …"

His words spluttered out.

"You made a promise to Simon, didn't you?"

Stephen Harris looked close to tears. "Will you have to go to the police?"

"I don't think that will be necessary," I said. "Writing poetry, as far as I understand it, is not a criminal matter in this country – at least not yet."

I tapped the folders.

"Is there anything in here that pours any light on Simon's death?"

He shook his head. "I don't think so. There's not a suicide note in there, if that's what you mean."

"Why the separate folders?"

He shrugged. "It's how they were given to me."

"By Simon?"

"Yes."

One of the folders contained poetry that had been typed out. The poems looked neat, possibly indicating final drafts. I could tell they were about someone close to the author, and I doubted anybody would be giving away prizes for guessing that Sharon McKenzie was the subject.

The other two folders contained a mixture of typed works with handwritten additions; and some handwritten fragments that looked messy, full of crossings out and alterations. I couldn't make much sense of the handwritten stuff and Stephen Harris wasn't much help on that score either.

I couldn't see anything in any of the poems that clearly suggested that Simon planned to take his own life, and I couldn't find a cry for help either. They were love poems, as far as I could tell. Sharon wasn't named in any of them, but she was there on every page, and quite possibly in every line.

"Stephen, are there any poems that you are not showing me?"

He looked on the edge of tears again.

"Only a few," he said at last. "I'm not hiding them from you – they're back home in Oswestry. There's nothing in them that I'm keeping from you. I'll get them to you as soon as I can."

I looked hard into his eyes and I believed that he was telling me the truth.

"Simon made me promise that his mother would never know about Sharon. I knew that the police would want to talk to me, so I made sure that his poetry was somewhere safe. He wanted me to have it. I haven't done anything wrong, have I? Will you tell his mother?"

"That's not your problem, Stephen," I said. "If she finds out – or if she doesn't – you've still kept your part of the bargain. Now, I don't suppose there's any chance of another coffee? That last one was made just how I like it. And why don't you have one yourself this time."

I looked again through the poems. It didn't take an English Professor to spot the change in tone.

"The boy was certainly in love," I said as Harris came back through with the drinks.

He didn't respond, and I wondered what a youth like him could make of such strong emotions so close to exam time.

I pushed the poetry folders to one side. "What else did he tell you about Sharon MacKenzie?" I asked him. "I get the feeling that she didn't get on with her step-father."

His face was a picture: a portrait in terror.

"Okay," I said. "You're not the first person today who's been reluctant to talk to me about someone named Cartwright. But I'm afraid that you're going to have to be the first one to take a deep breath and tell Uncle William what you know."

Harris took a drink of his coffee; and then he told me.

There was a visit one evening. A man in his late thirties, or early forties – Stephen Harris really had a taste for detective work, once he put his shoulder to the wheel.

Twist

The man came to see Simon. Stephen had been in Simon's room when the knock came at the door downstairs. The man, it turned out, wasn't the gregarious type, more the psychopathic type, only not quite so friendly. His presence hadn't indicated that he was paying a social call.

He asked Stephen to leave, and Stephen hadn't hung around for a second invitation. He'd sat in his room, looking out the window, waiting for the man to go. When he left, Harris went to check on his friend.

"I wanted to make sure Simon was okay."

"And was he?"

"I think he tried to play it down. But, thinking back, I think he was badly shaken up."

"Did he tell you what it was about?"

"He didn't tell me anything."

"Do you think it had anything to do with the girl?"

Harris looked away.

"Come on, Stephen," I said. "Let's hear it."

When he looked back at me I could see that the fear in his eyes had deepened.

I once read a description of someone's eyes turning to the 'colour of nightmare'. If ever such a description was apt, I was witnessing it.

This had nothing to do with keeping secrets from Beth Hilary.

I said, "Simon told you that the visitor was Cartwright, and that he was Sharon's step-father?"

The first tear was out and Harris was beginning to shake. I assured him that he was doing the right thing by telling me everything he knew.

Cartwright, it seemed, made a further visit a few days before Simon died. A week separated the two visits. If there were more visits, Harris didn't know about them.

"You don't know what it was concerning?" I asked him.

"I had my suspicions. I don't know that they're worth anything to you."

"Well, there's one way to be sure," I said. "But let me guess: you think she was pregnant?"

He looked at me like he believed I was a mind-reader.

"Elementary," I said, doubting that he would recognise the allusion. You just can't educate some people.

In a brief, self-satisfied moment, I imagined myself entering a lecture theatre, all cloaked-up, deerstalker and pipe in attendance, standing on the stage in front of a hall full of Stephen Harris clones.

"Look at it this way: a young and horny guy, rather like yourself starts seeing a girl from the local underwear emporium, and a little time later her step-father turns up. How many reasons can you come up with? Your time starts now."

I don't consider it my duty to convert the world to detective work. I am not an evangelist. But I do have my moments.

"You said that you were there on Cartwright's first visit, and that you knew about the second. Did you get invited to leave the room that time too?"

He shook his head. "I came back from shopping. Simon was in his room and I could see that he had been crying."

"You asked him about it?"

"He was reluctant to tell me anything. I asked if the man had been to see him again. He said that he had, but he wouldn't say more."

"And this was how soon before Simon took his own life?"

"Three days."

*

Before I left I looked again over Simon's last cache of poems. There was nothing that seemed to corroborate our mutual suspicions, though Simon did have an arty way of putting things sometimes. He could describe an apple and make it smell more like an orange.

In my finest Colombo style I made my false exit before turning around in the doorway. "Just one more thing," I said, scratching my head, and wondering if all of my dramatic timing was being criminally wasted. "Did Simon ever suggest that he was worried about his father?"

"In what way?"

"Did he confide anything about his dad being under stress – perhaps involving his work?"

Harris knew something.

I went back into the room and sat down. "In your own time and in your own words, Stephen," I said.

It took him a while to get his words out; and in the end, despite all of the stuttering and qualifications it amounted to no more than a handful of sentences. But once you assembled them properly they were interesting enough.

It seemed that Simon *had* been worried. That it *did* have to do with his father's business. That Simon had returned home one weekend, and was in the house when he overheard his dad on the phone. His manner on the phone had been different enough for Simon to move his ear a little closer and listen more carefully. He'd never heard his dad talk like that before. It was like he was afraid of something, or someone. And Simon confided to Stephen Harris that he thought someone might have been threatening his father.

"Can you be more specific?"

Harris shook his head.

"Was it blackmail?" I asked. "Simon's parents were wealthy, after all."

"He never actually used that word ..."

"But?"

"It's what I was thinking. It might have been what Simon was thinking."

"But he didn't say any more about it?"

"He never mentioned it again."

"Okay," I said. "Maybe that's enough for today."

I looked at the folders in my hand and wondered what Beth Hilary would make of her son's poetry, and of his secret life. And I wondered why she thought she needed to hire a detective to get a few poems back, and why Professor Potts had chosen to conspire with that when he would have been more than capable of performing that service for her.

I wondered what the two of them were playing at, and why it was me they had chosen to be here, asking these questions when I could have been perfectly content to continue with my uneventful life of humdrum surveillance and beer drinking back in Stone.

Stephen Harris was watching me intently in my momentary distraction. I caught his eye and suddenly he was looking scared to death, as though I was about to ask him some more about Cartwright.

"Do your best with the rest of the poetry," I said, and then I left him to his studies, hoping that the distraction wouldn't weigh too heavily on his future.

*

It was dusk when I reached the Oldcastle estate. If there was a moon out, it was lost behind the heavy banks of cloud rolling wildly across the sky.

I knew parts of the estate like the back of the legendary hand, having given a large part of what might have been the prime of my life to the place. It was a labyrinth, straight out of Borges. You could know it inside out and back to front and still become lost as easily as finding your way. Devils danced on pinheads and angels turned blind eyes and if you walked backwards you could turn the Ferris wheel around and lose five years without even selling your soul.

It had grown to almost twice the size that it had been in my student and police days. The old parts had stamped themselves across my psyche forever and would doubtless never leave me regardless of where life took me. It was a part of me and it would always be a part of me. But the new intermingled with the old and, like earlier in the day, I became quickly and inevitably lost. I wondered if that was my subconscious, the more rational part of my mind, protecting me: keeping me out of the jaws of the monster that lurked always in this sad and lunatic place.

Hopelessly lost, and with the night coming down thick and fast, I had no choice left to make.

Wherever the girl lived, nothing good could live.

Where had I read that? From between the covers of which lurid paperback had those words lodged themselves in the scrap yard of my mind?

In the real world, the good and the bad lived side by side, sometimes mixed together within the same four walls. This place though defied the rational part of me, and all logic and common-sense went off into the darkness on a child's drawing of a witch on the steps of a forest cottage.

If I had not found Sharon Mackenzie already, then I could not have found her that night. The better part of me would not have let me find her, here, in the descending darkness.

What lies I could tell myself, believing I was turning away from the heart of the place only to take on the labyrinth itself.

Oldcastle surprised me, as it always had done: this time letting me go without a struggle. I took it as a warning: it would not let me away so easily the next time, I was certain of that much.

On the outer rim of the estate, the night now black and cheerless, I sat in my car and thought about what Stephen Harris had said regarding keeping Simon's secret.

A girl from an underwear factory; a step-dad, brutal and squat, and likely as strong as an ox and five times meaner; a fear of the estate, of Oldcastle itself ... and yet Harris was not one to be drawn by that hideous charm that sucks the weak ones towards the darkness without them ever recognising the dangers.

It drew Simon and it had drawn me, many years earlier, but it had not and possibly never could draw the likes of Stephen Harris.

We remember the details of killers and concentration camps but forget the pleasant and the humdrum in our daily rounds. It was obvious enough to Harris that the girl and her family represented the underbelly of the shark that swims occasionally out beyond its natural habitat, entering the once-safe waters that society has declared home to the good and privileged that make up what we like to call the backbone of civilisation. To people like Harris it was like switching channels by accident and straying from the arts discussion on BBC to the switchblade rapist stalking the late hours on cable TV.

But where the likes of Stephen Harris would have turned back, corrected the mistake, or panicked and cried for help, Simon and I had lingered. Drawn to the darkness; hypnotised by the sparkle of dangerous eyes twinkling like demonic stars in the pitch-dark night.

Could it be that the death of his father had opened a small vent inside, allowing the darkness to seep and spread, contaminated beyond all hope, his blood in the water, the shark coming fast and furious?

I looked again at the poetry that Simon had written towards the end of his short life. It didn't tell me anything of sharks, of madmen, of curses upon the living. It told me only that a young man was, or had been, in love.

*

I drove back to town and parked up close to the Tavern in the Town. I was on time but Sharon Mackenzie was fifteen minutes late. I drank two pints of orange juice, and I was on my third when she came through the door and told me to make it a Bacardi Breezer for her.

We found a quiet enough corner, and then she told me that she couldn't stay long and so I'd better get down to business straight away. She appeared dressed for a night out, but clearly not with me.

I told her my business while she made short work of her drink.

"Get me another of those," she said, "and I'll tell you what you need to know."

Placing another of the same in front of her, and deciding that three pints of orange squash was enough soft drink for anyone, I took the head off a pint and pulled back my best listening ears.

Sharon Mackenzie wasted no time.

"It's Todd Cartwright you should be speaking to, not me. He's why Simon topped himself: *Todd fucking Cartwright*. We was alright, me and my mum, until she had to go and marry that bastard."

She was halfway down the second bottle already. I wondered if the revelations would dry up as soon as she reached the bottom, and that I would have to feed her like a meter to keep the information coming.

Her expression changed. "I'll tell you something and I'm not ashamed to say it: I loved Simon."

Her bottle was empty again. I asked if she wanted another but she said that she was meeting someone in town and couldn't stop. "Another time," she said. "Are you local?"

"Afraid not."

"Where you from?"

I told her.

"That's Simon's home town. You knew him?"

"Unfortunately I didn't."

"He was a great lad. If you didn't know him you'd say he was a bit stand-offish. But that's only because he was a bit shy. He talked a little bit posh as well, but that wasn't his fault. He knew where I worked and where I lived but he never once looked down his nose at me. I tell you, Cartwright ought to be hung by his bollocks for what he's done."

She stood up and straightened her skirt.

"Please," I said. "Before you go – I don't want to keep you – but what exactly did Cartwright do?"

"He fucked everything up, that's what he did. That's why I moved out. I left them to it ... the sad bastards. I said, if you want to dig your own fucking grave, then stay with Cartwright and rot with him for all I care."

"Did Cartwright threaten Simon?"

"He scared the living shit out of him. He thought he was being clever. Thought he'd found the goose that lays the golden fucking egg! Didn't occur to him that carrying on like that was going to make Simon either run for it or ..."

She sat down again. "Look, I don't mind talking to you. You seem alright. But I've got to be going, so how about another time?"

Her face had lost its hard edges and found itself breaking into a smile. "Are you in town long?" Her eyes had widened and were full of fun.

"Long enough," I said.

"Give me your number then."

I gave her my number and she said she would be in touch soon and then we'd have a "proper session".

And with that she was gone.

I ordered myself another pint.

NINE

Beth Hilary was asking for a progress report.

I drove back to Stone, to West Hampton, and straight to her mansion. I had Simon's poetry in my car, but I hadn't decided yet what to do with it. I wasn't sure how much of her son's secret life she already knew, and how much she had chosen not to tell me; and what secrets of her own she might be hiding.

I decided I would play it by ear.

She had a bottle of white wine going and said that she couldn't imagine that one glass would affect my professionalism. All the same, I declined.

The small talk lasted about as long as it took me to sit down.

"So, how's your investigation going?"

So: my quest for a few poems had already become redefined as an investigation. I didn't point out the distinction.

"It's raising lots of questions," I said.

"Oh, tell me more."

I watched her eagerly top up her glass.

"Simon didn't have to share a room," I said. "You could have provided private accommodation anywhere in the city."

"I could, that's very astute. But Simon wouldn't have allowed it. He always maintained that he didn't want any privileges. He wanted to succeed on his own merits. He was principled, sometimes quite ridiculously so."

"Do you think he had many friends?"

"He was his father's son. By that I mean that he was a loner. Terence knew a lot of people; he had to in his line of work. But he rarely made what I would call friends."

"And Simon?"

"Simon was the same in many ways."

She thought for a moment. "But ... having said that ... I would also say that my son valued other people; it wasn't just a case of what he could get out of them. He was shy; extremely shy, actually, and so naturally he found it difficult to make and maintain friendships."

Her glass was empty again.

"Terence was the same and it turned him into a workaholic. And being a workaholic doesn't leave you with much time for making real friends. He had a reason to call people if it was to do with business. But to call somebody up simply to tell them he was thinking about them, to check they were doing alright – he imagined they would doubt his motives. That's a man for you. I'd call it an affliction."

"And Simon inherited that?"

"How could he not?"

"I'm trying to understand your ... situation."

"We're not the Addams family! Ordinary people with an unfair slice of the cake, that's all."

The ambiguity of that last comment threw me as I wondered which cake she was referring to.

"Your husband made a lot of money."

"And every penny was honestly earned."

I couldn't tell whether she was being ironic or not.

"There's a lot of corruption around works of art, I believe."

"What are you trying to say, Will?"

"I have no reason to doubt that your husband was an honest man. But he must have come into contact with some less than scrupulous characters over the years."

She topped up her glass. "Of course he did. But he dealt with that by never compromising his ideals. The less than scrupulous know where to go and where not to go. If you always play it down the line you stop getting the sideways approaches. On the other hand …"

"Yes?"

"I'm not very good at this."

I wasn't sure about that.

After a long visit to the wine, she said, "I told you about my husband because I thought you might benefit from some background. On the other hand, I don't want you to waste all your energies looking into Terence's business."

"Was he being blackmailed?"

She looked shocked.

But not shocked enough.

"Are you talking about my husband's work?"

"Unless you can think of anything else."

"Meaning what, exactly?"

"I'm not trying to say anything particularly. You employed me to find out the truth, and that's what I'm trying to do."

"I employed you to find out about Simon."

I eased back in my chair. "What if Simon was being blackmailed?"

"That's absurd. Blackmailed about what?"

"With Terence dead, whoever was fleecing him might decide to move around the family."

"This really is the most ridiculous conversation," she said. "But if that was the case, just for the sake of argument, then it would make sense to come to me, wouldn't it?"

I let the unspoken question sound in her head, if it hadn't already. The one about where I was getting my ridiculous ideas about blackmail from.

She took a break. Said she wanted to get the fishcakes in the oven and hoped I was hungry. When she came back she poured again from the bottle, emptying it.

"I am not being blackmailed," she said.

"Not now, perhaps; but when Simon was alive – you would have done anything to protect your son. What mother wouldn't?"

She took on some more wine and I took a chance.

"Ralph Sterling died the same day Simon died."

She placed the glass back on the table.

I said, "Did you know that?"

"I don't want to talk about Ralph Sterling."

"He was your husband's business partner – is that right?"

"I said that I have no wish to talk about that man, not today or any other day."

"Was he blackmailing Terence? Did your husband commit suicide because of Ralph Sterling?"

"My husband's death was an accident! He wouldn't have done that to me – to Simon. His death had nothing to do with Ralph Sterling or anybody else."

She took a moment to regain her composure. More wine seemed to help.

"Let me be straight with you, Will. I haven't said this before because I thought it would put you off taking the case. That you might think me mad."

"Okay," I said.

"The last painting Terence handled made him nervous, and not because of anything to do with Sterling or blackmail or anything like that. There were people trying to drum up scandal, saying that he was dabbling in pornography, but he told them to go to hell, and rightly so. And when they came to me I told them the same."

"This last painting?" I said.

"It came from a collection owned by Aleister Crowley. You may have heard of him."

"Vaguely," I said. "Black magic, the occult - that sort of thing?"

"One of the world's most notorious black magicians, actually. He owned a castle in Scotland, and this piece of art that Terence was dealing with had once hung over Crowley's fireplace, according to the catalogue."

I tried not to let the conversation ruin my enjoyment of the promised fishcakes.

"Have I said something funny?" she asked.

"Not exactly funny," I said. "You're not telling me that your husband believed in any of that hokum? Unless it was good for business - putting a Scooby Doo angle on it. But in the episodes I watched, it always turned out to be men in rubber masks trying to scare off those pesky kids from finding out the truth."

"Have you finished? I'm not some mental case taking you on a wild goose chase. These are facts, Will. And that last painting – it made Terry extremely anxious. He wanted to get rid of it and he would have lowered the price to move it on. There was no funny business, not on our part, at least. My husband died without completing the sale, and so what am I supposed to think? All the nights lying awake, thinking about Terry, about Simon losing his father. I thought everything a person could think. I imagined *everything*."

Twist

We took some time out to do justice to the fishcakes. It was time well spent. She eased up on the wine but I could tell that her capacity might turn out to be legendary.

At some point it was time to get back to earning my living, and I brought up the subject of Professor Potts.

I said it was bothering me why he would recommend me rather than someone based in Leicester.

Beth Hilary merely suggested that I ask him myself.

I said that it didn't add up, and she agreed: nothing added up, which was why she had hired me. I was there to do the mathematics and *make* it all add up.

"He recommended you when I wouldn't give up the idea of hiring somebody. He warned me that most investigators would likely take my money and string me along for all they could get. He told me that you would never do that. And he was right, I can see that."

I didn't know what to say. I opened my mouth anyway. "How could he know something like that? He hadn't seen me for decades. And I was no great student."

"I don't believe you. I think ... once you put your mind to something, Will."

"That was my trouble," I said. "I was too busy putting my mind to too many things, chasing ... too many different forms of education."

"I'm sure that you have many tales to tell."

"No more than your average student away from home for the first time."

I saw the implications hiding inside my words. But it was already too late.

"I'm sorry," I said. "I didn't mean -"

"I have no doubt that Simon had his own secret life."

I didn't intrude on her comment, content to let it lie.

She waited for me, but when I tried to drink the nonexistent remains from the bottom of the glass of fruit juice that she had poured me to accompany my fish cakes, she said, "Simon was a young man and young men have their secrets. Why should my son have been any different? Maybe if I learn enough about the young student who was William Twist, I might discover the part of Simon that was hidden from me."

It seemed a strange notion.

I was still holding the glass up to my lips, and beginning to feel ridiculous trying to maintain the charade, when I finally gave in, placing the glass down.

"Knowing me doesn't tell you anything about your son."

I felt my neck start to contract, like I was trying to draw my face down into the space between my shoulders and hide it there. I was no agony aunt and no counsellor. All I could do was make both of us feel worse.

"We don't know anybody in this world," she said. "Not even our own flesh and blood. We don't even know ourselves."

For a moment I thought she was going to cry, but then she startled me and laughed instead.

"Look at me! Now *I'm* beginning to sound like a philosopher!"

Then, abruptly, she stopped laughing, and said, "Have you found Simon's poetry?"

The question needed an answer and it needed one fast.

I made the decision to present her with the complete works of Simon Hilary once I had it, and then I told her that I was hopeful that I'd get a result soon.

She didn't believe a word of it.

"What haven't you told me?" she asked.

I said, "Simon never had a girlfriend?"

"Those things would have come, given time."

"Perhaps," I said, "if Simon had a girlfriend, she could tell us things that could be illuminating."

"What ... that a man always confides his deepest secrets to a woman – is that what you're suggesting?"

"It sometimes happens that way."

"Well it didn't in this case!"

The way she said that, the force and venom behind the words, rocked me back in my chair.

I said, "I'm sorry. I'm not trying to upset you."

"I'm sorry, too," she said. "I didn't mean to … I'm sorry."

I jumped in with both feet on the back of her apology.

"Are you saying that Simon couldn't talk to you?"

"Of course he could talk to me – I'm his mother, for God's sake!" She shook her head. "He could talk to Terence about anything."

"But not to you?"

"Do you have to be so brutal? There was no girlfriend that I knew of."

Her eyes could pierce tank armour.

I thought of Terence Hilary; and I imagined a man who had looked into those eyes and crumbled.

What if he had attempted the impossible? What if he had embarked on some course of deceit and sought to conceal it from her?

"Do you need more money to get my son's poetry back?" she said.

"No."

"Are you sure?"

"I'm positive."

"Good," she said. "You're the only person left that I can trust."

*

That night I slept like a bluebottle in autumn.

I came across that line in a book about a man full of foreboding because time was running out and he still had to kill his wife and make it look like kidnap.

It's not a book I could recommend even to someone I didn't like. But I liked that line. I think the follow up was something about a dying insect having bad dreams. Mine, though, were all to do with my dead mother's new habit of writing stories of my life from the grave.

In my dreams she'd written a new collection. The first story, from before I was born, explained why I had been drawn to Leicester.

As a young woman, she had unlocked a casket of evil buried deep in Oldcastle soil, and in manhood I would have to end what she had started and put that evil back down in the hole where it belonged. Otherwise my life would continue to slip into the darkness of an ancient nightmare that only I had the power to end. Except that I was becoming less heroic, running from the climactic fight, and bringing death and damnation to everyone I had ever known and loved.

I'd always enjoyed a happy ending.

TEN

Roy was at the office early and he seemed to be full of good humour.

"The wife's looking forward to seeing you," he said. "I think she wants to give you some good mothering. It's your favourite, too, and with all the trimmings."

"I have heard rumours," I told him. "Don't tell me she's started cooking already."

"She's a perfectionist, Will."

There was no disputing that. I could see the beef joint in my mind's eye; and I could almost smell it too. My teeth were grinding at the thought.

Roy assured me that he was alright managing my cases. But then Roy would say that. He would have told me he was managing even if it was keeping him awake every hour of the night. The force should have cried buckets the day he left, but I knew better. The kind who will do anything for anybody, not because they want to be seen in the right light when the promotions are doing the rounds, but because they give a damn about the public they are supposed to be serving, and about their colleagues too – that kind are treated every time as mere cannon fodder.

I'd first met Roy on the beat in Leicester, and though he rarely set foot outside Stone these days, he kept in touch with some of his mates who hadn't made it to retirement yet. So when I told him about Todd Cartwright he said that he would cash in a few old favours and see what was on record.

He took out a folder, and I could see he'd been busy alright; and so had Cartwright.

"He's a right case, Will. The Oldcastle boys would love to nail him. There's a string of domestic incidents with the ex-Mrs Cartwright – he put her in hospital twice. He co-habits these days with Sheila MacKenzie and her daughter Sharon."

"Have either of them got any previous?"

"Doesn't look like it though Cartwright more than makes up for them. He's done time, but not nearly enough of it."

"What's he done time for?"

"Let's see now." Roy flicked through the printouts and notes. "We've got some GBH – football connected, and there was a nasty incident outside a nightclub. He nearly killed a youth in an argument over a dog. And talking of dogs, there's a suspended sentence for organising dog-fights. Numerous cautions for anti-social behaviour, both in the local neighbourhood and in the town centre. There's an appearance pending at the magistrates for incitement to cause a breach of the peace outside a football ground. Some coded stuff too – unfinished."

"How about extracting money with menace?"

"There's plenty of that. He fancies himself as a regular *Godfather.*"

"In Oldcastle they call them *Step-Fathers.*"

Roy laughed. "Have you met him?"

"Not yet. But it's always nice to have something to look forward to." I nodded towards the notes he was holding. "Anything else to report?"

He flipped the pages. "There are quite a number of dropped charges ... some of this stretches back years. He's a career criminal all right. Good at putting the frighteners on by the look of it, a regular enforcer. Not exactly Don Corleone, but nasty enough."

Roy had a few of my other cases to sort before he'd earned himself a Friday pint, so he didn't hang around in the office. On his way out he advised that I ate nothing until Sunday, and I vowed to live like a saint until we met again. But I was never the best at keeping those kinds of promises.

*

I made some calls and arranged some local visits. Before I left the office I shared a coffee with Angie, and she asked how the case was going.

I thought that she looked concerned.

"What is it?" I asked her.

"I don't know, Will. Something's bothering you. You don't look right to me."

"Perhaps it's this new haircut I'm trying out. It's hard to get on with I'll grant you."

I laughed but she didn't laugh with me.

"Perhaps it's being back in Leicester," I said. "Too many bad memories, like I told you."

She didn't say anything.

I tried again. "How about taking too much money for trying to find a few poems? It's too easy."

Still she didn't say anything; she just looked at me.

"It's just too easy, Angie. And it doesn't feel right."

"What isn't right?" she said.

"Nothing's right. I wish I hadn't taken this case."

I noticed the time and said I had to go.

"Do you trust her?" she asked.

"You mean Beth Hilary? What are you saying?"

"A feeling, that's all."

"A woman's intuition? Come on Angie, what is it?"

She took a breath, and finished her drink. Her eyes remained fixed on the empty cup in her hands. "I've been reading about her husband's death. I remember the story on the news. I've been checking out some stuff."

"I see. Looking for a promotion to detective partner, eh?"

"When she came into the office the other day."

"What?"

"I should mind my own business. Stick to what I'm paid to do."

"You think she killed her husband?"

Angie looked at me, obviously shaken by the abruptness of my question. "Be careful, Will," she said, placing her hand over the back of mine. "Just be careful."

*

I drove out the few miles to Stafford, where I was due to meet Graham Tilburn.

Tilburn had dealings with Terence Hilary stretching back years, and it looked like he'd done almost as well for himself.

We sat in his conservatory, with gentle classical music playing in the background; it seemed to be soothing the cows grazing calmly in the fields that stretched endlessly behind the property.

"Straight as a die, Terence was. Not a corrupt bone in his body."

I hadn't suggested otherwise and I wondered if Tilburn was reciting a code that all practitioners of his craft had to sign up to. It wouldn't be a unique state of affairs for a professional body to close ranks in the teeth of a scandal.

I asked if he had ever been to the Hilary house.

"Once or twice, yes. His wife was utterly charming. They were so devoted, you could tell that a mile off."

Tilburn seemed to have a habit of answering my questions in advance of me asking them, as though the object of the exercise was to allay any suspicions and hasten my departure. If that was his plan he had a lot to learn.

We spent some more time establishing that Terence Hilary was a perfect guy with a perfect wife and a perfect life to match.

It was time to shift gears.

"What about Ralph Sterling?"

Tilburn's comfortable leather chair seemed to have become notably less comfortable. "What about him?" he said.

"You knew him?"

"I did meet him, briefly."

"In London?"

"I believe it was at a dinner party at Terence's home."

"What did you make of him?"

The chair was becoming more uncomfortable by the minute, and so was Tilburn.

"You didn't like him?"

Tilburn shook his head. Maybe the admission that someone in the business of art was less than perfect was a step too far.

I laid out some facts that he already knew: that the rumour-mill was suggesting Sterling was likely the victim of an organised hit, and that Terence Hilary had been Sterling's business partner for some considerable time.

I tried my best to help make any admission as easy as possible for Graham Tilburn, and he repaid me, eventually, though the process proved as difficult work as delivering a baby with twelve heads.

"... Sterling was, shall I say, at times a rather ruthless businessman. Terence could be, too, but not in the same way. There was something - how do I put this? There was something rather *dark* about Ralph Sterling."

"Can you be more precise?"

"I don't have anything specific to tell you, Mr Twist. But rumours in the business suggest that a number of people had their fingers burned dealing with Ralph Sterling."

The baby with twelve heads was beginning to come out, and I slipped on the rubber gloves and got ready to pull hard.

"How did Sterling get on with Mrs Hilary?"

"I don't think she liked him, frankly."

"But Terence liked him enough to make him his business partner?"

"I'm not certain 'like' is the correct word. They were both driven businessmen, and I imagine what they had, first and foremost, was a business arrangement."

"Did Ralph Sterling have anything on Terence Hilary?"

"I don't know what you're saying."

"Did any of the rumours around Sterling include blackmail?"

"You're asking if he was blackmailing Terence?"

"Was he?"

"Regarding what?"

"You tell me, Mr Tilburn."

"I have no idea."

"Did Terence have any weaknesses?"

"What kind of weaknesses?"

"Gambling?"

Tilburn laughed. "Terence – gambling! He was too tight-fisted to take a chance like that. He only bet on certainties, or tried to. Like any decent businessman."

"What about women?"

"What about them?"

"Could he have been having an affair, perhaps, and someone found out?"

"Not that I'm aware of. I didn't know him well enough, as I've already told you. But I'm not ... as far as I know Terence and Beth were happily married. That's the impression I had anyway, for what it's worth. Like I said, they seemed devoted to one another."

Watching him carefully, I said, "Simon Hilary died the same day as Ralph Sterling."

Tilburn didn't bat an eyelid. "I knew it must have been around the same time. I didn't realise it was the same day. What are you suggesting now, Mr Twist?"

I wasn't suggesting anything. I was pressing buttons and seeing if any of them were wired up. But the baby with twelve heads was putting all of those heads together and playing with me, demanding that I earn the designated part of a small fortune left over from recovering a dead student's poetry.

I pressed at some more buttons, and at last I hit one that made Graham Tilburn's chair become uncomfortable again.

"Beth Hilary is quite an artist herself," I said. "You must have seen some of her work when you attended the dinner party."

Tilburn didn't say anything.

"Now, I'm not much of an art critic myself, but I'd say that some of her work was a little on the weird side. Did you know that her husband was dealing with art works that she believed had occult connections?"

I could see that he didn't want to answer me. But the question wasn't going away, and neither was I. At last he said, "As I indicated to you earlier, Mr Twist: Mrs Hilary was charm itself -"

"But?"

"Well, okay, what I mean is … I think Terence was a little embarrassed by her sometimes."

"You don't share her belief in the occult?"

Laughter clearly came as a great relief to Tilburn, and he luxuriated in it. It stopped him moving around in his chair and upsetting the leather. It also got the twelve-headed baby in position. I was ready and waiting.

When he'd finished laughing and realised that I wasn't joining in, he said, "Terence spent a lot of time in London."

"Are you telling me he didn't like spending too much time at home with an 'eccentric' wife?"

"I'm not saying that. But, well, yes, there were whispers going around that she'd told other people similar things, presumably at other dinner parties, or whatever."

"And so Terence preferred to conduct business elsewhere?"

Tilburn took a moment. He was getting ready for that final push to be rid of that dozen-headed fiend inside him. He looked at me, as though making certain that there was no other way of getting me off his back and out of his property. With those final checks completed, he said, "There was a rumour."

"What rumour?"

"That Terence and Beth were separating."

*

I drove out of Stafford for my appointment with Jason Hadgett, who had not only known Terence Hilary, but who had been involved in his final dealings, and therefore with the art work that convinced Beth Hilary that the devil was alive and well and setting up home in North Staffordshire.

Hadgett was a good deal younger than Tilburn, though by my estimation he was probably only a handful of years from a conservatory looking out on endless fields of gently grazing cattle.

We started off covering much the same ground that I'd already covered with Tilburn, who he knew but hadn't seen in a while. Hadgett didn't have any noisy leather chairs that made him uncomfortable, but he did have a wife who knew how to boil a kettle and keep the biscuit plate filled up.

"Terence had a good reputation. He was very good at his job and you could trust him. I don't think his partnership with Sterling did him any favours. Sterling was a different personality. Got popped, didn't he?"

"I believe the police are still looking into it."

"I think there was a lot of dirty stuff going on there."

"How dirty?" I said.

"Sterling wouldn't turn down anybody's money. I heard his partnership with Terence was putting a strain on the marriage. Mind you, what I heard about her, maybe he was better off out of it."

"What did you hear?" I asked him.

"Well, you know. It sounded to me like she was a bit of a flake. A very nice woman, by all accounts – don't get me wrong. Bit of a stunner, too. But I heard she was making noises about the deal we were involved in, and even tried to get Terence to drop out."

"Was Ralph Sterling involved?"

"No, not at all; he was busy down in London, where he did most of his work. Mostly this one was dealt with in Cheshire. I didn't have a lot to do, but I did spend a weekend in Altrincham, and Terence was around for at least the Saturday."

"Did he talk to you about his private life?"

"Why would he?"

"Did he talk about Sterling?"

Hadgett looked puzzled. "What are you getting at?"

I ignored his question and asked some more of my own. But in truth they were shots in the dark and there was nothing even in the echoes. We called it a day and I thanked him for his time.

I was almost back in Stone when the car ran me off the road.

*

A face I hadn't seen for a couple of days and hadn't missed at all, glared at me from the comfort of my own passenger seat.

"So what do we know about Terence and Beth today then?"

DI Sykes was wearing a car coat that looked borrowed from the set of *The Sweeney*. It suited him.

I gave him the fruits of my time with Graham Tilburn and Jason Hadgett, and then I asked him what he thought of me driving around Staffordshire doing his job for him.

He seemed satisfied that I wasn't holding out on him and suggested I stuck to retrieving student poetry at inflated prices.

As he was getting out of the car, I said, "Whose death are you interested in, really?"

He sat back down. "Remind me," he said. "What are the options?"

"Ralph Sterling," I said. "Terence and Simon Hilary."

"And what's your theory?"

I suggested that Beth Hilary had killed them both and then tried to make her son's death look like suicide.

That's when he grabbed me by the throat and said that if I ever took the piss again he'd *cut my fucking dick off*.

Then, straightening my shirt for me, ever so gently, he asked if I had further business in Leicester. I told him I was still chasing down the poems.

He didn't even smile. He got out of the car.

Before he closed my passenger door he leaned back in and said to me, "Let me save you some time and effort, Mr Twist. Terence Hilary slipped off a rock in a blizzard and died a needless and tragic death. Ralph Sterling was killed by a professional hit man and I'm not really fussed who pulled the trigger or who hired the hit. I'd call it a public service myself, but don't try quoting me. Simon Hilary killed himself."

He stood up straight "There. I've been more than generous. Good luck with the poetry and good day to you."

He closed my door and walked away.

ELEVEN

I drove to the university on spec. Professor Potts was available to see me. I went into his office and took my customary seat, overwhelmed again at the vast library of philosophy surrounding me.

He asked how I had got on tracking down Simon Hilary's poems, and I told him that I was still working on it. He was looking a good deal perkier than I was feeling; and in case he was in the mood for more games I got straight down to business.

"Beth Hilary didn't know that Simon had a girlfriend. At least I don't think that she did. But you knew."

"Is that a question or a statement?"

"Which would you prefer?"

His sigh was heavy and ponderous. "I suspected as much."

"You don't think it would have been useful for the detective you recommended to know that?"

"I didn't *know* and Simon never told me. I merely suspected the presence of a woman in his life. I did not and do not wish to burden you with my personal suspicions. I have no wish to mislead you."

There was no point arguing. Potts hadn't lost an argument in his adult life. Professors didn't lose arguments they merely blamed their adversaries for not fully understanding the issues.

"So that's what I'm doing here?" I said. "Finding out what you already know so that I can tell Beth Hilary and save you the hassle?"

The pause stretched but Potts didn't seem the least bit uncomfortable with it. It was an act of mercy on his part when he said, "It surprised you that Simon had a girlfriend?"

"It didn't surprise you?"

"Should it? Few young men venture into university life for the sole purpose of hearing an ageing professor rambling on. That's a conceit I ditched only too recently."

"You said that Simon was single-minded, incapable of distraction."

"Oh, dear," he said.

"What?"

"I fear that I'm being misquoted. As I understand it, nobody is entirely incapable of distraction. I recall our last conversation quite clearly. I suggested that this was indeed the case, but *prior* to his father's death. We can only speculate as to what factors conspired to distract Simon, and in what degree, though I cannot contain the idea that his father's death did not have a profound effect on Simon."

There was a jingle somewhere in his voice that said this was all playtime to him. Nothing malicious, just the cerebral masturbation that keeps an academic sane.

I didn't comment, leaving the ball in his hands, doubting he'd take it any distance.

"You don't think," he said, "that Mrs Hilary would approve of Simon having a relationship? Or are you protecting the dead boy from some form of posthumous shame? I would imagine that, at some level, she knew. Women, particularly mothers, tend to have a nose for this type of thing, so I'm told. It has something to do with maternity, with the maternal instinct, I believe."

"Would you say that Mrs Hilary is rational at the moment?"

He weighed the question so carefully that his face seemed to move from side to side, as though internal scales were shifting to find the point of balance.

"If you're asking if I think that she's mad, then I would most definitely have to say not. I would be amazed however if she could possibly be functioning in a way that could be entirely defined as normal – whatever in Christendom that might amount to."

"She seems to give some credence to the idea that her late husband's work might have brought bad luck on the family."

Potts laughed. "That doesn't sound like you talking, Will. If I might be so bold, it sounds more to me like a carefully worded understatement."

"I'm not sure what you mean."

"It might sound strange if you start banding words like 'occult' around. You don't want me to think that *you're* crazy, after all. And, sorry to disappoint you, but I would not so readily dismiss Beth Hilary's thoughts as simply the results of too much grief born too quickly."

I wanted to say something, but I had temporarily become incapable of forming a sentence. My face was no doubt doing its best to express more or less everything that was at that moment hurtling chaotically through my head.

Potts, meanwhile, was regarding me carefully, no doubt weighing up whether it was safe to put his thoughts into words without the risk of me running from the room screaming for help from the troops dressed in white coats.

"Listen to me," he said. "You're not here to look into any of this. It is not what you do and Beth Hilary should not expect it."

I returned the scrutiny, watching him sitting in his director's chair, hands clasped over his knee. I was looking for signs. It seemed to me that we were edging towards a moment of revelation, and, in my experience, they usually came gift-wrapped in layers of non-verbal information every bit as revealing as the words spoken.

I'd lost track of whose turn it was to speak.

Beth Hilary had told me about the work her late husband was involved in before his death. Potts was right. I didn't want to get into any of this. I tried to put the brakes on. I had no obligation here, yet I was fast becoming lost in a different game, as we sat on our respective perches, and eyeballed one another.

"I thought maybe she was trying to intrigue me," I said. "Keep me interested in the case. Why else would she tell me about her husband's art dealings?"

I waited to see what response came back, but Potts merely shrugged.

"I wouldn't know about that, of course," he said. "We all have our ways and means, no doubt. When you first came to Leicester, I recognised a quality in you that I had observed in myself many years earlier, and that I saw again in Simon Hilary many years later. Do you know what I'm talking about?"

"I'm not sure that I do."

I saw his chest rise with the extra breath, and I took it as a sign of exasperation.

"I'm talking about the thirst for understanding. I'm talking about the need to reach beyond, to something higher, brighter; something un-nameable, and quite possibly unreachable. It was in you, and so I recognised it. Let's go back to our friend Wittgenstein.

"When all questions that can reasonably and sensibly be asked, have been answered, all the interesting problems and mysteries of our life and this world remain untouched.

"It's a poor paraphrase of what the great man said, but it will serve us for now. He was a detective and that's why he read mystery books. He recognised the important fact that he too was a character in a story. We all are. But we are all different and no doubt capable and called to play many parts. But paradoxically we can only be defined by – we can only fully *inhabit* - one kind of story. Most of us that is."

I said, "I haven't read that in the commentaries."

"You're not likely to. It owes more to my own understanding of the world. What Beth Hilary wants from you is entirely mundane, though it may still save her from hell."

"I'm not following you."

"Some minds, in the face of mundane realities, take flight to higher and lower realms. Others, catching glimpses of heaven and hell, content themselves for all eternity with a faithful marriage to the mundane. You're the detective, and I don't believe that mankind has yet come up with a more absorbing occupation. Life is one huge mystery on so many levels, and all thinking men and women are detectives; they have to be to survive. The true enquirer into the heart of the world, the person of scruples, of moral worth who conducts his life so that he can illuminate only the deserving mysteries – that detective represents the greatest that we can ever aspire to be."

"You mean a philosopher?"

"You can use whatever term you prefer. I don't think it really matters. Wittgenstein is remembered as a philosopher; he read detective books because he was a detective. You want to know why I recommended you ... haven't you worked it out yet?"

"No," I said. "I always was a poor student and I still am. You'll have to spell it out for me."

"I don't believe you," he said. "You just want to hear it from me. The detective in you rules the roost. It's what you were born to do. I recommended you to save a grieving widow and mother from madness. She doesn't believe that the police did a thorough job and she can't dismiss the idea that they may have missed something. She wants her mind putting at rest. She needs somebody to take her seriously. Someone with integrity and compassion – and someone who can assure her that everything has been properly looked into. Then she has a chance – an outside chance, perhaps – but still a chance of closure."

It was a quality performance. But I still didn't trust him. I said, "Were you aware that Simon might have been under pressure from his girlfriend's step-father?"

"Pressure to do what?"

"I get the impression the step-father isn't a nice man, and that he may have seen his step-daughter as a meal ticket."

"Do you imagine that all roads lead to money?"

"Most of them seem to, in my experience. You're not aware that anybody was intimidating or threatening Simon?"

"I'm not. Simon was deeply troubled and in need of solace, no doubt. If he was being intimidated or threatened, as you say, then he never confided that fact to me. If he had done then I would have passed that information on to the police."

"Did you meet Terence Hilary?"

"I did not, unfortunately."

"Why do you say unfortunately?"

"Any man who could raise a son like Simon, and attract a woman like Beth Hilary, must have been a man worth knowing."

"Have you heard the name Ralph Sterling?"

"I read the papers and I occasionally turn on my television to watch the news. It seems that this person may have been somewhat disreputable in the world of art dealing, and that he may have paid the price for that with his life. That's all speculation, of course. I am not privy to special knowledge in the matter. I'm simply reading between the lines: a passive recipient of the media available to me."

Whatever he knew or didn't know, I was dancing to his tune. Yet I still couldn't see the angle he was coming from. It was there, lurking in the shadows; and I caught glimpses out of the corner of my eye. But I was damned if I was getting any closer to actually seeing it.

We called it a day.

There was a missed call on my phone from Sharon Mckenzie. She had left me a voice message, wanting to see me. She would be in the Tavern.

I checked my watch.

As I stood out in the weak sunshine I watched the students drifting back and forth across the campus. A part of me was longing for the past and another part was glad to be rid of it.

I had an urge to call again on Stephen Harris. I doubted he would have had chance to get the rest of the poetry, but there was something chewing away at me all the same.

With exams looming I was confident that he would be sitting at his desk. He didn't seem to get out much.

I drove back to the blocks and it turned out that at least I had one hunch right. And as I had expected, he didn't exactly look thrilled to see me.

"I haven't had chance to get the poems," he announced as he opened the door. "Like I said, they're back in Oswestry -"

"It's okay," I said. "Don't worry about it. Can I come in?"

His expression changed from trepidation to curiosity. He wanted to ask me something and I invited him to take the opportunity.

"Did you have any luck with Simon's girlfriend?" he said as we went into his room.

It seemed on the face of it an unfortunate manner of speaking; but I was sure that it wasn't intended that way.

"Nice girl, unfortunate family," I said. "I found her quite helpful."

I could see that he was itching to ask me more.

While he was busy framing his question, I took out my pen and wrote down my office address. "You can forward the rest of the poems to me whenever. I doubt it's urgent. And if your student loan's troubling you, don't bother with the stamps – we'll pick up the tab."

"You're satisfied it was suicide?" he said.

"Aren't you?"

He looked away.

"Stephen?"

"I was hoping," he said.

"Hoping what?"

"I don't know."

"That there was something more to it?"

He nodded, weakly. "I suppose so."

No doubt he wanted some of what Beth Hilary wanted: a reason, solid ground; something tangible to rage against and to smash at least a metaphorical fist into. The stupid, pointless waste of his friend's life was too much to accept; too raw; too, well, *pointless*.

"The man," he said, and he seemed to almost choke on the word.

"Todd Cartwright? I doubt he'll be coming back to see you."

I watched some of the load shift, but not all of it. I took my payment for that by asking another question: the one that had been brewing since I left the company of Professor Potts.

"Do you think Cartwright wanted a shotgun wedding? Or do you think he was just a bounty hunter hoping for a break?"

Harris seemed a little unclear about what I was asking.

I said, "Do you think she was pregnant?"

"Simon didn't say anything about that."

"So Cartwright was an opportunist trying his luck?"

"Simon's parents were rich. If Sharon McKenzie knew about their wealth ... I don't know, I'm only guessing."

At last somebody had voiced it. No bullshit, just plain old fashioned motive that never changed down the years.

"Thanks for your help, Stephen," I said. "And good luck with your exams."

"I'll send you the poems," he said.

He was still holding onto the paper with my address. The window above his desk was open.

"I would put that away somewhere safe before the wind takes it out of your hand," I told him.

He glanced out through the window. The trees in the distance were standing straight and untroubled. "There isn't any wind," he said.

"Let's hope it stays that way."

I left him alone with his puzzled frown.

As I walked out to my car I looked up at the sky. It was impossible to call.

TWELVE

I walked into the Tavern and ordered a beer. It wasn't the elixir of life but it felt good all the same. It had been a long time since I'd sat waiting for a date of any kind to walk through the door, and Sharon McKenzie was becoming a regular habit.

I ordered again. Already she was forty minutes late. How long should I give her: one more drink, or sit quietly and wait until the hour was up, and then what?

I really was out of practice.

I watched the door until *she isn't coming* became *she's coming but not alone.*

My imagination was firing on all cylinders: she'd told her thug of a step-father all about the snooping detective who needed teaching a lesson not to go poking his nose into other people's business. Todd Cartwright was on his way with a pit bull terrier straining at the chains that rode the calluses of his monstrous strangler hands.

My drink was gone and I could feel the ball in my stomach start to empty the sweat down the back of my neck. I should get out of there fast, relocate to the pub across the road and observe who came in here. Had I learned nothing from all the hard-boiled heroes I'd studied so religiously in books and films? Had my education amounted to ... *this*?

I stood up, placed my glass on the bar and turned to leave.

And in she walked.

"Sharon!"

She was alone. I glanced toward the door. Was Cartwright outside, his gang revving up the dogs for an early summer barbecue of uncooked flesh?

"Looks a bit crap in here tonight," she said. "Fancy moving on?"

Where to, I wondered: through some dark alleyway to the land of fists and knives?

"Okay," I said. "Show me the sights."

She grinned and headed back out into the street.

I followed.

In the jaws of the enemy I would make smart remarks to my grave so that they could say 'he died a hero, a wit, a *character.*' But the autopsy would reveal the truth. They would cut me open and see the yellow running from head to toe and back up again. They wouldn't find a single joke worth the telling in there and the bones wouldn't impress a scrap yard mutt.

We walked into The Hillgate. It was my first time. I don't know what it had been in its previous life – a drop in centre for junkies and child molesters by the look of it.

Sharon walked up to the bar and ordered me a pint. I silently vowed to switch to soft drinks.

I reached for my wallet but she insisted. I asked if she'd eaten and we agreed on an Indian. The food in The Hillgate was the condemned prisoner's last meal, and he was welcome to it.

She suggested a drink in what she called the bar on the road out of town.

The Bohemian.

How could I refuse?

As we walked under its shadow I expected the ghosts of my past to tear out through the doors and finish the job from all those student years ago. My visit with Carl had provoked the spirits from the past and given them time to assemble. I was back in my mother's fairy tales.

"Not here," I whispered under my breath. *I will eat everything off the menu back at The Hillgate - but please not The Bohemian with a girl from town.*

The gods were smiling. Sharon McKenzie was starving.

We passed beyond the shadow and on to the Indian.

*

The bottle of house red didn't last, and Sharon ordered another. I promised myself one glass more before the shutters came down and my internal bar was closed up for the night.

But now she was talking about Simon.

If I sat cold and sober listening to her, all I would be short of was an open notebook and a pen. *Just a few notes, miss, you understand. Nothing formal, just establishing whether you or a member of your family were responsible for killing your boyfriend.*

She finished her meal and filled up both of our glasses, telling me how different Simon was to all the others. She had only been out with lads from the factory, or from bars and clubs in town. Simon came to her from another planet.

"You should have been there when he first spoke to me. We were in the 'French Rev'."

I knew the French Revolution; I recalled my time there only too vividly. I had lived through it. It had taken me to my hell.

" ... I was with my mate from the factory. We were thinking of calling it a night. They were playing all Sixties shit and I was knackered. When I saw him come in with a couple of skins, I thought I was hallucinating."

"He came in with skinheads?" I asked her.

"We knew them but we never had anything to do with them. Skins aren't my scene. Too fucked up, excuse my French."

The laughter shrieked out of her.

"Simon had been around a few pubs, trying to get away from students, he reckoned. Paul got talking to him. I used to know Paul before he started messing about with the skins. Paul was alright back then, but anyway: he reckoned he'd sat next to Simon in the Unicorn and he reckoned student straight off – it was so fucking obvious, everything about him. But Paul said he was a right good laugh so that was okay. I mean, Simon was about as streetwise as a poodle: a student walking into a bar full of skinheads! I mean, he almost deserved a kicking for being so stupid. Anyway, he told Paul straight out he was at the Uni, and it takes some bottle coming out with that in the Unicorn, I can tell you."

"What happened?"

"Paul said he just loved the bloke for that. He'd never come across anything like it. So he buys him a drink, asks if he fancies keeping it going, and brings him over to the Rev."

"Was Simon drunk?"

Sharon didn't answer. When she started up again, her tone was more thoughtful, reflective.

"He was dancing. He looked so unlikely in there that I said to my friend that I was staying for a bit longer. I was ... fascinated, I suppose. Then I got up for a dance. Paul was dancing with Simon, well not exactly with him, I mean, neither of them were queer, nothing like that. The skins were around the bar, planning their football violence for the weekend like they usually did. Paul caught my eye but he knew better. He could see I had my eye on his mate and he gave Simon the nod.

"He was a bit shy, so I made it easy for him. I moved right up and gave him the eyes and everything. I could see one or two of the regulars looking at him, wondering what he was doing in there. He was so out of place you wouldn't believe it. But I was known in there so there wasn't any danger of anyone starting anything. And anyway, Paul wanted to get back into my good books."

I looked at her questioningly.

"Paul had some hold over the skins, and if someone needed seeing to, he could get it arranged with a glance and a flick of his fingers. I've seen him do it. It was like some weird magic he had. But if somebody needed looking out for – it worked both ways."

"Sounds like the mafia," I said.

"It was just like that. If you saw him – I mean, Paul's the same build as Simon, not exactly an athlete. He didn't look tough but he knew people. And he knew what to say. When you're dealing with people like those skins, you don't have to be anything more than a dog-handler – then you can form your own army."

I watched her fill both glasses again, and I was relieved that the bottle was empty. I doubted she would order another one as we had already asked for the bill.

" ... What made Simon so different," she said, "he wasn't either all over me or taking it the other way and doing all of that super-cool shit. I could see in his eyes that he fancied me rotten. And he had the nerve to look at me. He loved watching me dancing. I've got a good body, if I say so myself, and I can move it around a dance-floor. He appreciated me and I tell you I could have torn his clothes off there and then."

She restrained herself, so the story went, and took her little-boy-lost home to meet Ma and Step-Pa.

"The morning was so funny. We were squashed into my single bed and Mum came in with my cuppa like she always does, bless her. She's alright is my mum. Got her problems, but, anyway ... Simon's hair was a bit straggly before I got him to have it cut, and it was about the same length and colour as Paul's. Mum looks down at his head and screams, 'Get that bastard out of that bed and out of my fucking house now!'"

Sharon shrieked again with laughter as she recalled the moment.

"I tell you, you never saw anyone look so scared in all your life. He shot out of that bed, his skinny arse pointing at my mum as she stood there with a mug of tea in her hand. I thought she was going to throw it at him. He was struggling trying to get into his pants. I thought I was going to laugh myself sick."

She shook her head at the memory and then washed it down with another glug of wine.

"Anyway, when he finally gets his pants on and turns around and Mum could see that it wasn't Paul, she treated him like a long lost son: bacon and eggs for breakfast, the works. See, the trouble with Paul was that, apart from having no prospects and no desire to ever get a job, he once came around asking for somewhere to stay, and we couldn't shift him for two months.

"But that was when Mum met Todd. She was trying to make a good impression, though God alone knows why she bothered trying to impress a piece of scum like him.

"Anyway, Todd had one of his *quiet words*. Can be very persuasive, can Todd. He's a right rough bastard. Makes Paul look like a saint – makes most people look like saints, if you want my opinion. He's just scum all round."

"Your mum approved of Simon?"

"She thought her little Sharon had won the fucking pools. Nothing too much trouble for her prospective son-in-law, and she was forever telling me to get him over for tea so she could show him a tin of salmon or something. That was her idea of putting on a spread, bless her."

"Did he come over?"

"Are you kidding? Simon saw the funny side, but you can take a joke too far. He only came around one other time, and that was when I got flu. He brought me some flowers. That's how sweet he was. I tell you, Mum thought her little baby had died, gone to heaven, and taken her along for the ride. He never came around again though. I think that tin of salmon was past its sell-by date."

The wine was gone and I was trying to catch the waiter's eye. I wanted to keep the momentum going, but not the booze.

I was about to ask for a coffee to add on to the bill, when Sharon said, "Fancy a move across the road? Bohemian gets lively on a Friday. Be a good laugh."

The waiter came over. The word 'coffee' slipped away from me and the word 'whisky' stepped into its place.

Sharon said that she was feeling adventurous, and she decided on an Indian brandy.

I did what I could to wrestle the conversation back to Simon, but I could feel a weight over my shoulder.

The prospect of a visit to The Bohemian with a girl from town was getting the better of me. That and the cleavage Sharon was revealing. Either she'd adjusted her clothing and I hadn't noticed, or the huge meal she'd tucked away had expanded her flesh and given the illusion that her clothes had shrunk. It may even have been the booze affecting my perceptions.

She was asking if I'd been with a lot of women. I took a hearty taste of whisky and tried not to choke on it.

"Some," I said, the tears in my eyes coming from the whisky and not the recollections.

"I think you're being modest," she said, her eyes twinkling. "What do you look for in a girl, anyway?"

I started laughing, and then I took on some more whisky.

"Come on," she said, "Don't you be shy with Sharon now."

"I like a good conversation," I said.

She smacked my arm. "Don't be boring. I reckon you're a tit man myself."

"I have been called something similar," I confessed, "but not recently."

"So who's your dream date?"

"You, of course," I told her.

She pushed out her chest. "I said you were a tit man."

Our voices had risen and I could see the couple in the alcove opposite glancing over.

"Let's get the bill," I said.

"I was only fooling," she said. "Don't take it so seriously." She swilled down the brandy. "Come on then, let's pay the man and get over the road."

*

Outside in the night air I could feel the booze. But still I wondered how I was going to walk through the door of that place, grinning at us from across the road, without a pint of something substantial inside me.

We started crossing and I tried again to get Simon back on the agenda.

"So, anyway, what about Simon?" I asked her. "What did he like about you?"

She started giggling. "Do you really want to know that?"

"I wouldn't ask if I didn't."

"He liked my shy personality."

Her giggling reminded me of a cartoon character that I couldn't quite place. It was cute and infectious though I had no doubt that it would eventually drive me to distraction. Not that I intending being around long enough for that to happen.

I wondered how many men had shared that thought.

"Simon liked ... you'll laugh when I say it."

The comment jolted me out of my reverie.

"Laugh?" I said. "Why would I laugh?"

"He said he liked my face. He said it was the most beautiful face in the whole world."

"That's one of the most romantic things I've heard."

She punched my arm. "Are you taking the piss?"

"Why would I do that? He was obviously a man of considerable taste."

"You are taking the piss!"

She punched me again as we stepped back onto the pavement, this time most definitely on the wrong side of the road. The Bohemian seemed to rise up in front of us and growl down with grim forebodings. I had no doubt that it remembered me, and not merely from my recent visit with Carl.

"I think you're a bit of a lad on the quiet," she said, and then she punched me a third time.

We weren't even inside The Bohemian and already the violence was beginning.

*

The pub was busy, but there were a few vacant seats scattered here and there. A lot of people seemed to prefer standing in the middle of the large bar room area. Sharon said it was her round as I'd bought the food.

I asked for a pint of bitter and then I found a seat and let the ghosts start to assemble around me.

The barman was the same one who'd served me and Carl, but nobody else looked familiar. I tried to remind myself that twenty years is a long time, and to re-assure myself of the impossibility of walking through that door to find everybody suddenly stopping drinking, all eyes on me, wild west style. It was just a pub. What happened there could have happened anywhere, in that city or any other. We would drink and we would move on. There was no significance. Ghosts don't exist, we conjure them. We tie a person, or an event, to a place and it remains that way forever.

It was likely that I alone in the world remembered what had once happened there. I alone gave it significance, and gave it life.

She came back with the drinks, joining me for a pint of lager by the look of things.

"Did Simon drink lager?" I asked her.

"Not a big drinker, Simon. Shit!" she said. "You wanted bitter."

"It doesn't matter. Simon didn't drink?" I asked her.

"You're not going to ask me to compare you or anything weird like that?"

"No," I assured her. "That's something you grow out of."

"Simon liked to keep a clear head for his studies. I think the embarrassment of our first night put him off booze for good."

"Waking up at your folks' house?"

"Not just that. Sex, I mean. Like Simon was really up for it, but not up, if you know what I mean." She was giggling again. "Like he was shaking that much, trying to get my clothes off – I thought it was going to be over before it had started. You ever had that problem?"

"Not for a while," I said.

"But then he couldn't do it, and he started crying. I did my best to make him feel okay about it. But when he stopped crying he started throwing up. And then I knew it wasn't going to happen at all. It was nice just being in bed with him, though, and I didn't think that would have been any fun at all. You live and learn don't you?"

The giggling had stopped and there was a faraway look in her eyes. I realised, unlikely as it might be, that this short-lived relationship had been the real thing, for Simon and for Sharon. It had been love and nothing less.

She was giggling again. "But the first time proper – I tell you, he made up for it. Hadn't had any experience, you could tell that, but he was as keen as anyone I've met. He'd be so horny he couldn't ever make the first one last. Until I taught him a few tricks."

I could only begin to imagine.

"The time he cried?" I said, my drink almost gone already, hers too. "Did he cry much? I mean, about his father? Did he talk about his dad?"

"I could tell he missed him. Like I missed my own father when my mother told him to fuck off and never come back. But I suppose it's different when somebody dies. I mean, then you know there's never any coming back."

"Do you know what Simon's father did for a living?"

"I know he was interested in art or something like that. I don't know much about it myself."

The pub was filling up now. It was getting noisier, and I was having difficulty catching everything she was saying.

We were back out on the street, then on to another pub. She insisted showing me the French Revolution. I should have confessed to having already been there in a previous life, but something stopped me. Perhaps it was the thought that one lie revealed would prematurely end the evening that kept my mouth shut.

She told me that the club stayed open until everybody was too pissed to buy any more. I said that they wouldn't have to wait too long on my account.

After we'd left The Bohemian she seemed to find it increasingly difficult keeping her mind and conversation off the more basic aspects of life, including the tricks she'd explored with Simon. I battled on regardless and, before we reached the French Revolution, I was rewarded with a labyrinth of sentences, spread out like an ancient puzzle, suggesting that she knew Simon was coming into a "shit load of money".

The night was making sense at last.

My mind flipped back over the sentences spun over thousands of words, the countless drinks and punches to my now bruised shoulder. I dug out the gemstones, the nuggets buried in that wobbling mass of an evening; the shining lights emerging in flashes from hours of digression, the wild shapes of juxtaposed fragments that somehow, miraculously, drew a picture so clear at last that even my booze drenched mind couldn't help but see it.

Todd Cartwright had a nose for money, and he wanted a piece of the action. And when Sharon's mum found a pregnancy testing kit in her room, Cartwright was already through the door and heading for Studentsville.

"... All that was missing was a fucking rifle under his arm. He had the brains of a sewer rat. I hate that bastard. He ruined everything."

We were in the centre of the floor at the French Revolution, dancing to something slow and obnoxious, my arms wrapped around her. She was telling me that I reminded her of Simon and I wasn't putting up any argument.

"I wanted to go to Stone. I bet it's cool there. I wanted to see where he lived. So did Todd, the bastard. He wouldn't leave him alone."

We danced. And she kept on talking.

"Stone and the Uni," she said, dreamily. "And you were at the same one?"

"It was a long time ago," I said.

"It shows, though. I can tell you've been educated. Sharon doesn't miss anything."

She looked up at me as we lolled around the dance floor to another slice of tedium that ought to have been consigned to the bin marked 'weddings'. A grin gleamed across her face like a sunrise. "You really do remind me of Simon, you know that?"

*

The rest is a haze. How we got from the nightclub, I simply don't remember. Where we got to … that's the part I do remember.

Fragments: walking into the house, heading upstairs, Sharon holding my hand, gliding me upwards; watching her undress, watching her dancing by the bed. I might have been dancing too; watching her move, falling onto the bed, giggles and laughter, references to Simon and how he had done it like this, tried to do it like that; puppeteering my hands around her as though they belonged to her dead lover; comparisons, electricity rising above the alcohol yet failing to provide the vital surge; falling headlong into darkness to the fading, distance sounds of scornful laughter; then waking and wondering if all this had been more dreaming ... wondering if loneliness and frustration had taken me to the bottom of the pit, trying to pick up the perks from the dregs of somebody else's tragedy ... opening my eyes and seeing her standing there, kneeling there, lying there ... feeling my hands on her body and hers on mine, the nightmare beginning again and the weakness of my flesh conspiring with the emptiness of my soul ... the sudden shiver of coldness, hearing voices, feeling so scared that I thought I was going to lose all control ... reality bursting in ... this wasn't some sordid dream, we were in her bedroom. The voices from outside the room: a woman shouting in a fifty-to-sixty-cigs-a-day rasp. *Sheila Mackenzie*. And the answering bell, like something salvaged from the bottom of a river: *Todd Cartwright*.

Sharon had been wrong about him. He didn't sound so much like a rat as a pit-bull, and an angry one at that.

She was looking at me with a stupid smile plastered across her face. "Fucking hell," she whispered. "Better keep your head down. And whatever you do, don't tell him you're a friend of Simon's."

"What are they doing here?"

"They live here. They must have come back early from Blackpool."

"You said you didn't live with them anymore."

"I don't. Any more questions?"

The night had passed, and the morning had come screaming in. I got out of bed and fumbled at my clothes. I could hear giggling behind me as I stepped at my underpants at least half a dozen times before I managed to get the things roughly where they belonged. If Todd Cartwright was about to come bursting through the bedroom door, I at least wanted to be covering the family jewels, grubby though they had become.

Or, rather, hadn't.

She whistled. "I tell you what: you should take to drinking shandy you wimp. What a letdown!"

I never realised how many buttons dotted my clothes like landmines to sabotage me. I fumbled and wrestled until I was looking, if not feeling, almost respectable.

"And here's me beginning to think I should go out with more students! All that reading gives you some ideas and no kidding. But then it all goes limp and you'd rather get a good night's sleep. You don't know what you missed and you never will."

Any other time, any other place, and Sharon's deprecations would have served as fatal blows to my ego. But at that moment I was temporarily liberated from the sin of pride, my thoughts focused entirely on the bedroom door, and the silent prayer repeating in my heart that might keep the thing shut until the sound of those hellish voices had gone and I was off that estate.

I wanted to be beamed up to the mother ship. My work there was done. I could, within two hours, find myself in a semi-civilised pub in Scolders Rise, lifting a pint to Roy and Carl, and promising that one day I would tell them what happened.

I heard the door slam downstairs and looked out the window to catch my first sight of Todd Cartwright.

From the back he *did* look like a pit-bull; a pit bull complete with bristle cut and commando jeans. A white Mike Tyson with a tyre around his middle and doubtless a few less quid in his pocket.

I watched him march away out of sight, and imagined the frightened Simon Hilary listening to those army boots marching all the way up to the door of his flimsy, poorly defended student block.

The door burst open behind me.

"What's he doing here?"

"Mum, it's the weekend."

"I want him out, weekend or no fucking weekend."

It was the end of a beautiful friendship.

But Mrs Mackenzie obviously knew best.

The door slammed behind her and I looked at my watch, like I was remembering an urgent appointment on the other side of the moon.

"Ignore her," said Sharon.

"I'm not sure that's wise."

"Come on," she said. "Get those clothes off and come here."

I wondered if this was just another Saturday morning in that house.

"I have to be going," I said.

"That's it, then?"

"Sharon ..."

"Don't Sharon me. Nice tits, but not good enough for you university types? You couldn't hold a candle to Simon. You think I'm some slag who works in a factory, but Simon loved me. He said it sober and he didn't have to. And if it wasn't for this bunch of losers that call themselves my family, I would have had his baby and he would still be here and ..."

She broke down. I stood watching as she sobbed; impotent in word and deed; and then the spell broke and I moved towards her. "Sharon ..."

"Get away from me."

The door swung open again. Mother MacKenzie was looking about ready to ignite.

"What you doing to my baby – I told you once, out that fucking door. Todd'll be back any minute, and if you're still here he's going to bastard well kill you."

"I'm going."

"You'd better be. Todd'll skin you alive."

It didn't seem the time for heroics. I looked back and found myself wishing to God that Simon Hilary was still alive and had this girl with him, and their baby. I could have wished that he'd never had to make that Friday night

148

journey into town; that he'd never had to know the names Cartwright and Mackenzie. But, God help me, I didn't wish that.

*

Walking along the road, I had the choice to turn right or left. It probably didn't matter, but at the time it seemed like a life or death decision. I had a plan: I would get on the first bus or hail the first taxi, and ask to be taken as far away as they were allowed to take me.

To my left I could make out a distant figure moving in my direction. It resembled a charging bull, and all that was missing from the scene was a storm of dust being kicked up by the furious stampede as Todd Cartwright's ugly features came slowly into focus. He had a newspaper under his arm, not a shotgun. I was more or less certain of that. I decided not to stop him and ask directions.

In the books I was reading I would have played it cool, not merely asking directions, but riding the moment; engaging him in a chat about the April weather and his plans for the summer. Did he prefer his Wimbledon afternoon strawberries with cream or knocked-off Guinness?

That he did not know me from Adam – and likely didn't know who Adam was – would not have saved me from death or serious misadventure had my accent reminded him of the student who once came to his house, loving his step-daughter for who she was and not because he was endeared to his future in-laws. The student who, in the boiling brain of Todd Cartwright, was not flesh and blood and never had been; rather the golden goose: the fortune that had slipped away forever.

And somebody had to pay the price for that.

Somebody was already paying and would never stop.

I turned from this charging animal, and into the strengthening wind that was spitting drops of rain into my face.

Goodbye Oldcastle and goodbye Leicester.

But it didn't turn out that way.

THIRTEEN

Walking had never felt better. I navigated the riddle of the streets, and though they seemed endless, and likely turning me around in circles from which there was no escape, the motion was affirming: *at least I was still alive.*

At some point I checked my phone. It was switched off. I booted it up, and for a moment I thought I had my bearings. It turned out to be an illusion.

It also turned out that there was an urgent message on my phone to ring Angie.

From my days with the police, I retained a residual fear of the word 'urgent'. It was one of the many scars the job had left in some dented crevice of my mind.

I wondered if Carl had been busy in the art world, conjuring spooks in the name of Terence Hilary. Or if Mrs Meredith had overdone the roast potatoes and, perfectionist that she was, had asked for a postponement of the feast. But the internal jokes wouldn't take hold, and a hollow pit opened up in my guts.

An urgent message from Angie.

I made the call.

*

The world had changed. The world was less of a place today than it had been yesterday.

I found a taxi to take me back to my car, and then I jumped in behind the wheel, and pointed it in the direction of home.

I was dreaming, that had to be it. I was living out another variation on a story my mother wrote a long time ago.

But where would I wake up: in the bed of Sharon McKenzie, or in Scolders Rise, perhaps, with Beth Hilary and her dead family nothing but a nightmare conjured by an over-active imagination?

I was going to the Meredith house to partake of the great feast; except there would be no feast, not now. How could Mrs Meredith recover from this? How could any of us recover from this?

Roy had been out visiting one of my clients, when the driver of a transit van pulled out of a side street.

Roy didn't stand a chance.

It happened while I was walking into the Tavern in the Town, ordering my first pint on a Friday night; waiting to meet the woman who had conceived Simon Hilary's child, and then who had proceeded to destroy it. And while I had been sleeping the sleep of the damned in Sharon Mackenzie's bed, taking the perks of the job, or almost, rare as they might be, Mrs Meredith had been rehearsing her goodbyes to the man she loved.

If I had been where I belonged, it would never have happened.

Roy was tired, working too hard to try and keep a sinking business afloat. Alert, he would have seen the van, and been able to avoid the collision. But if I had been back in Stone, he never would have been on that road at all. He would already have been at home, his wife taking the lid off the Friday evening casserole, and Roy kissing her, the two of them making plans for great things when he finally retired and gave her the attention she deserved.

If I hadn't made that phone call to Angie, the world would still be revolving around my dilemma about what to tell Beth Hilary. How to hand her son's poetry over to her, whatever it told or didn't tell and whatever she already knew.

*

I pulled up outside Angie's house. She'd just got back from the hospital. She threw her arms around me while Carl stood behind her shaking his head.

When Angie finally let me go and went to the kitchen to make a drink, Carl asked how the case was going.

"Who cares?" I said.

"Listen," he said. "I want you to remember something."

"About me being noble and righteous ... *all in the line of duty*?"

"Roy wanted you to take the case."

"Save it for another day, will you."

Carl grabbed my shoulders and pushed me hard against the wall.

"Roy doesn't need your self-pity and neither do we," he said.

"Fair enough," I conceded. "But do you want to know what I was doing last night – how I was spending my evening?"

Angie was shouting from the kitchen, asking what we were drinking.

"Surprise us," Carl shouted back, his weight still pinning me to the wall. Then he said to me, "I don't care what you were doing or how you were doing it and Roy wouldn't either. He was proud of you, proud to have you as a colleague."

"Proud to know that I was back in that city trying to relearn how to be the same waster I was all those years ago?"

He eased back as Angie came through from the kitchen with a tray of hot drinks, though I was never to find out exactly what was in those tall steaming mugs.

"Are you two lovebirds sitting down for these?" she asked.

The three of us sat down while Carl and I stared at each other until he said, "Okay, whatever else is on your mind, for God's sake let's hear it."

I said, "Do you think this was an accident?"

Carl edged forward in his seat. "What are you talking about?"

"It could have been a warning."

"Are you being serious?"

"No," I said. "It doesn't make any sense."

"What are you getting into, Will?"

Then Angie's voice cut in, something about food.

I turned to her. "How's his wife?" I said.

Angie was saying something about people coming out of comas, regaining consciousness. But I took it as nothing more than the etiquette of preparing for a funeral.

I stood up and left.

*

I drove to the hospital. Roy was in intensive care. His wife was sitting with him.

They told me I couldn't go through to see him. I got as far as the window outside his room when they turned me back. I could see Mrs Meredith holding his hand. I couldn't see Roy's face but I could tell that he wasn't moving.

As they ushered me away I saw her turn around. Maybe she heard the slight scuffle going on, I don't know. But she looked at me and a smile lit up her face. I thought that smile was going to break my heart.

*

154

I drove back to Angie's and the three of us sat around in silence. Then someone started talking again and Angie said that Carl and I were welcome to stay the night. There was a spare bed and a sofa.

We sat staring at the television and drinking tea. A comedy show came on but the lame jokes only made me angrier.

I kept repeating my own question: *accident or warning*?

But this wasn't one of those polished-up prime-time thrillers where nothing happens without a reason; this was real life. There didn't have to be a *reason* why Roy was fighting for his life. It was just the way that the world sometimes likes to conduct its business.

I said I was going to head back home for a while, and that I might catch them later.

I went back to the hospital. Mrs Meredith was still there. Staff I hadn't noticed earlier were milling around and I tried my luck again. But they still wouldn't let me through. Again I got as far as the window to Roy's room, and then they were pushing me back and threatening to call security.

Mrs Meredith appeared at the door and walked back down the corridor with me to the coffee machine. I asked her a hundred stupid questions and all the time she looked solid and strong.

She told me to go home, and she was about to go back to keep her vigil when I asked her to say hello to Roy for me. I felt foolish saying that, and she told me that we mustn't give up hope because Roy would never give up hope if this had happened to any of us.

I left believing this to be another part of the etiquette, another part of the grim preparation for what was to come.

I was never the best when it came to saying goodbye.

*

The next day I was in the office trying to sort out what needed to be done, and getting precisely nowhere.

I went through to reception. "Is it break time yet?"

Angie looked at her watch. "It can be."

"Pub?"

"Why not?"

"Put the calls on divert."

"Thanks for the advice. You do employ me as secretary, in case you'd forgotten."

I drove up to the village and parked outside The Three Legged Dog. I hadn't used the place in months.

Angie commented on how quiet it always was around Scolders Rise, and I said that was likely due to the residents staying home to butcher their families in the comforts to be found only behind closed doors.

She thought I was tough on the place and I agreed that I probably was. She asked if I'd ever considered moving and I told her the truth: that I loved the peace and quiet but hated the peace and quiet.

I told her that in all the years I'd spent living there I'd never got to know anybody. She asked me if that was a positive or a negative and I said that I still hadn't decided. That I was working on it and likely would be for the rest of my unnatural life.

Angie was drinking tonic water and I thought that a beer couldn't inflict much more damage on the already bruised day. We sat out at the front on one of the benches provided, while a weak sun fought to show itself through a determined show of cloud.

Somehow we got onto the subject of my family, my all-absent family. Mum, Dad, Carol and Josie. I'm still not sure which one of us brought it up. I wondered if Angie felt sorry for me. I hoped so. It would be one more thing that we had in common, that and watching the ship we were on going down.

We ordered sandwiches and chips, though most of it was left uneaten. The clouds seemed to multiply and thicken, and I could feel a storm building.

I suggested we move inside to finish our drinks. But Angie said it was time to get me home. I said I still had work to do, and she shook her head and said, "Not today, Will. You were useless before you had three pints. I can't see your performance improving now."

I was walking toward my car. But Angie stopped me; said we should walk. She was right, as usual.

We walked the few hundred yards towards my house, the thunder growling above us and forks of lightning spearing the leaden sky. Then suddenly the sky unloaded.

The deluge appeared almost biblical.

By the time we reached my road the rain was coming down so hard that it was difficult to see more than a few feet in front. But running down that hill, splashing our way towards my front door, was exhilarating. As I forced my key finally into the lock, we were laughing our heads off.

We were soaked to the skin, her clothes clinging to her. I said there was an old hair dryer that might still work, and that she could borrow a dressing gown while her clothes went in the tumble dryer.

I headed upstairs to change. I didn't hear her footsteps behind me.

I was getting out of my clothes when she came into my bedroom. I picked up the towel I had thrown on the bed, and held it around myself. She was wearing the robe I had lent her, wearing it open. We moved towards each other, and then time and space slipped, and we were on the bed. It couldn't have been too long after that that we found ourselves sitting up, looking awkwardly at each other.

I wanted to ask her what the hell was happening. But it hardly seemed polite.

She said that she really ought to be getting back to the office. Her hand touched mine and I let the moment pass. Then I felt her hand leaving mine.

Her clothes were more or less dry, and when she'd dressed I called for a taxi.

The rain had stopped though the sky still looked full of it. We heard the taxi pulling up outside and she looked like she wanted to say something.

I watched her hesitate in the doorway and the words 'can I get you another drink?' formulated in my head but went unspoken. I stood in the doorway watching her getting into the back of the taxi, and felt the last chance to open my mouth draining into the gutter with the remnants of the storm.

I waved. I don't know if she saw me, if she was even looking. I closed the door and went back inside the house. The whole thing felt like I should have been soaking in the bath, dreaming it the way I had done so many times before.

I went back inside and sat on the couch, my head in my hands, wondering if this was the beginning of the end, and that my time working with three good people was drawing to a close.

I remembered the evening we went out, just before Christmas. The four of us on our own works party. We all had a few that night, with Angie celebrating the last part of her divorce, toasting us, her partners in crime, with a gin and tonic in her hand. We all but convinced ourselves that evening that we were turning a corner, and that the fates were on our side. That the coming New Year would see our fortunes change.

And we had all raised our glasses.

FOURTEEN

I was passing the retail park. There was a large toy store close to the entrance. I drove to it and parked up. It was five to the hour when I walked in, and they looked about ready to ring the bell and pull down the shutters.

I was feeling like a contestant in a game show.

You have thirty seconds, Mr Twist, to find the special present and take it to the till. If you succeed in this you can make the princess smile again and that is tonight's star prize.

On cue a voice came over the loudspeakers, instructing the punters to get a move on, if using fractionally more sensitive language.

I raced around the aisles, almost blind in my panic to buy something, the right thing. All I could see were rows of cheap plastic, including a bizarre section of dolls that looked intimidating enough to keep a gangster awake for a month. Josie's birthday wasn't tomorrow, not even that week, yet I had a strong – no, *urgent* compulsion to buy something that night.

Retracing my steps back along the same rubbish-filled aisles, some pock-faced youth with a strong local accent reminded me that the store was about to close, and would I please start making my way towards the tills.

I glared at him until he backed off, and then I walked into the adjacent aisle.

There were toys there that I hadn't noticed on my first pass, or possibly I had missed out that aisle altogether. One or two of the items looked a little more promising.

The voice over the speakers gave out its final warning while I was looking at a dolls' house, all boxed up.

I wanted to look what was beneath the packaging. But a voice behind me was telling me that the store was closing. I turned around to see another pock-faced youth with an even broader accent. The place seemed to be practically teeming with them, and I wondered if they ran on batteries. I told him that I was well aware that the store was closing because at least half the store seemed to be employed for the sole purpose of informing me of that fact, and why was he holding me up telling me this again when if he just left me alone I would make my choice and then we could all go home.

I took the box off the shelf and walked to the tills, the staff, the security guards, waiting for me like I was a shifty looking Colombian carrying a stringed parcel towards passport control.

*

Out in the fresh air I knelt down by the side of my car and threw up. I took some deep breaths and leaned against the bonnet.

I could see one of the security guards watching me.

I unlocked the passenger door and tossed the package inside, feeling a little easier. The illustration on the box did look impressive. Josie was going to love it.

I turned to see the guard still watching me. "It's okay," I shouted. "I'm alright. But thanks a lot for your concern."

I sat in the car trying to get the cogs of my brain moving again. I felt like somebody had reached a hand inside my skull and wiped away the facility for memory and logic. Was this how senile dementia begins – or was this the start of a mental breakdown ushering in through feelings of sad confusion and a pulsing emptiness?

Twist

I looked again at the gift next to me on the passenger seat, and I took refuge. The illustration on the box was really something, and I felt a warmth radiate through me as I imagined Josie opening it.

Gently I prized open the box.

There must have been some mistake.

What were these scraps of coloured plastic? They didn't correspond with the promises beautifully depicted on the packaging.

I got out of the car. This needed clearing up.

I walked to the entrance, but the security guards were waiting to turn people like me away.

Tweedle Dum and Tweedle Dee informed me that the store had now closed. But they didn't understand. I held up the box and I showed them the contents. I asked them if *they* would have been satisfied. They - one appointed spokesman and his faithful nodding dog - suggested unanimously that I come back in the morning.

That's when the tears started, and they hadn't paid for tickets to see that.

I threw the whole kit and caboodle down on the ground in front of them, and roared out my unrighteous farewells to cover the grief I was feeling.

*

I drove to Angie's house. She made coffee, and as we sat together in her living room, sharing that big, comfortable sofa, she told me that Roy's wife still wanted us to turn up tomorrow as arranged. It seemed ludicrous, but then on reflection it seemed the only sane thing to do, and I promised that I would be there.

As I drank my drink I looked at her and said, "I'm sorry about, you know - what happened earlier."

There was a long, uncomfortable pause. I was almost at the point of asking her if she'd heard me, when she said, "Are you?"

"No," I said.

"Good. Neither am I."

Angie didn't need any more pain and suffering, didn't need it any more than the rest of us. She'd had her share, more than her share, and this house, this lovely home on the canal side, was testament to the hell that she had once endured from the business man husband who had left her with it as dues for being caught like a rat in a trap.

Angie had lived at the end of the rainbow until one day the sky went black. That was the price she had paid for being a devoted wife and an aspiring mother. The knock at the door in the middle of the night. Her husband's lover fearing that he had taken another woman onboard - and what did she propose to do about that! A year of shock and anger mixed with counselling and tablets and solicitors and regrets, and then it was time to take stock and to finally move on. An ad in the local press hiding beneath a coffee cup one afternoon: three unlikely detectives trying to earn a living on Stone High Street and needing somebody to organise them. A marriage finally made in heaven.

We finished our drinks. After a while she said, "I think Carl wants to talk to you about the business."

"Stuff the business," I said.

"That's what Carl says."

"You could be out of a job," I said.

"I'll find another. Or else I won't. I'm not exactly going to starve to death."

I kissed her. "I'll see you tomorrow," I said.

"We're meeting at noon. If you come here just before, we can all travel over together."

"How is she?"

"As well as can be expected. But this isn't the hardest part."

"She's a good woman," I said, "and solid as a rock. They deserved each other."

"This isn't your fault, Will," she said. "These things happen. They're unfair, unjust, but they happen. Roy wouldn't want anybody else suffering for it, and certainly not you."

"Justice," I said.

"What about it?"

"There doesn't seem to be much of it about."

*

I went to see Carl. He lived a few miles out of town in a property he was renting from an estate agent who owed him a few favours. We ended up drinking from his collection of bottled beers and we ended up drunk.

We were talking about Roy, remembering our times together. Talking like he was already gone.

Somewhere in all of that remembering, I said that Roy should have gone to Leicester instead of me.

"What good would that have done?" said Carl.

"He would have been better suited to the task."

"Why?"

"Less baggage for one thing, and anyway, he was the only man of integrity around."

"Thanks a lot," said Carl.

"He wouldn't have got distracted. He wouldn't have gone loaded with other agendas. His bullshit detector ..."

"You're starting to sound like an old record, Will, scratched and warped at that. You were the man for the job, and you've done the job. It's not your fault the way things turned out."

"Then whose fault is it?"

"You found the poems and you found the truth. It wasn't nice, it wasn't even dramatic. There was nothing particularly original about it, either. Squalid and tragic but still the truth. And you got to it. You did what was asked of you, more than was asked. What more could you do than that?"

I shook my head. "I've done nothing more than peel back part of the scab. There's more to it. There's a lot more to it."

"Like, for instance ..?"

"Potts is hiding something."

"That makes no sense, Will. Why would he recommend you if he knows something but doesn't want you to know? If he's hiding something – what's the sense in that?"

"I don't know. Appearances, maybe?"

"Being seen to be doing the helpful thing?"

"Possibly," I said. "Or he thinks it's better that it's me looking into this than someone else. The two of them, Potts and Beth Hilary ..."

"You think there's something going on?"

"There's certainly something. But what kind of thing?"

Carl smiled; the smile of the true cynic. "Well," he said, "I'm sure we could narrow it down easily enough: how about sex or money - or both? What else is there? You thought something was off from the beginning."

"I didn't know the half it and I still don't."

"Maybe they conspired to see off Terence Hilary and pocketed the insurance money."

"And then hired me to look into it?"

"Okay, so what if she killed her husband and the Professor's blackmailing her?"

"Then where does Simon fit in? He caught wind of it and topped himself? And what about Cartwright? He was intimidating Simon, but I can't see how anyone could

164

prove that led to Simon taking his own life. I should have stayed out of it."

"Roy wanted you to take the case, you know that."

"So everybody keeps reminding me."

"He even checked out Cartwright for you. He wouldn't have done that if he hadn't approved. Are you going to pass any of this on to the Oldcastle boys?"

"What's the point? There's not likely to be any evidence that Cartwright was trying to extract money with menace. He visited Simon alone."

"Stephen Harris saw him."

"But he didn't witness what went on. There was no evidence of violence. And any threats made were heard by Simon and no-one else."

Carl thought for a minute. "What if Potts really is the genuine article, trying to help the maiden in distress? Perhaps he knows how to tie all this up in a bundle that you can present to Beth Hilary. Or simpler still, you could leave her with the poetry and call it a day. It's not your problem. If nothing else, Roy's wife is going to be glad of the money your work has raised. Not entirely wasted efforts, Will."

We kept on drinking and talking until at some stage we fell asleep or else passed out. When I woke up it was morning. Carl was already in the shower and my mind was circling around what I was going to say to Beth Hilary.

But first I had to work out what I was going to say to Mrs Meredith.

*

We picked Angie up and arrived at Roy's house on the button. Mrs Meredith greeted us at the door as though nothing had happened. It was hard believing that Roy wasn't home, uncorking the wine, running around the kitchen with his best apron on so that Carl and I could make facile remarks like a couple of schoolboys.

Mrs Meredith was fighting hard to keep upbeat, and Angie kept asking questions about how she'd made the gravy, the sauce, and the dessert-to-die-for. I kept looking at the place where Roy's chair should have been, wondering what *he* would have done to set the record straight with a scumbag like Cartwright. How *he* would have handled the Professor's half-baked hints that something bigger than greed and ugliness was behind it all.

The afternoon passed, and some relatives from down south turned up, and the remains of DMT said our goodbyes.

Mrs Meredith hadn't mentioned Roy all afternoon, but before we left she rang the hospital.

There wasn't any change. I said I would run her there, but relatives were taking care of all that.

Carl and Angie said they were calling for a drink. I didn't feel like drinking. I said I wanted to go home and that I would call them later.

*

I drove to the hospital. This time they let me into the room. His wife was sitting with him and the relatives were taking turns.

I sat looking at Roy, not knowing what to say or what to do.

Mrs Meredith went to get a drink, and when she came back I said that I had to go. I touched Roy's hand ... and in that moment I felt everything changing.

The world tilted, and dimly I caught the true shape of it: I could no longer play the part of some soft boiled Hamlet taking forever to decide whether or not to act.

In that moment of awakening I heard Mrs Meredith ask how my little girl was doing, and I left before the tears came.

*

I drove. It seemed better than drinking, and foolishly I thought it would leave the door open for some light to come pouring into the darkness.

I found myself, intentionally or otherwise, passing the Hilary house. Not believing in coincidence, I guessed that at least my car knew where it was going. I parked up next to the Mercedes convertible and apologised to my jalopy for my insensitivity. Then I got out and rang the bell.

The door opened and Beth Hilary looked out on a wild stranger.

"Will - are you okay?"

I went inside.

"I've had some bad news," I said.

"Can I get you a drink?"

"No, thanks. I'm not staying."

"Bad news?"

I told her about what had happened to my friend and colleague, and the next thing her arms were around me and I could have been her son back from the dead.

"Are you sure I can't get you that drink?"

I shook my head and swallowed hard.

"What is it?" she asked.

"You know about Simon's girl, Sharon McKenzie; and Todd Cartwright. You know that Simon was going out of his mind thinking he still had to get a lousy First because it's what the Hilary family do – it's what's expected."

She gave me the benefit of the doubt. "You're upset," she said. "You need to get some rest. We can talk about this another time."

"No," I said. "My mind has never been clearer. Simon couldn't let the family down, not a family that built its house on the wrong kind of foundations."

"What are you talking about?"

"Do I have to spell it out to you?"

"Maybe you do."

"Okay, so here it is: I'm talking about fraud, perhaps – or how about blackmail?"

"I know you're upset, Will - but have you lost your mind?"

"You really don't know how your husband made his money, his *real* money? I think Simon knew. I think lots of people knew, including whoever was blackmailing Terence. And I think Simon knew about the blackmail."

"I think it's time you were leaving."

I shook my head. "Not yet. I haven't finished. Terence liked to keep his name clean and respectable. But someone did their homework. I don't know who and maybe it doesn't matter. Simon overheard a call. Days after that call Terence was dead. Simon lost his father, and out of desperation he confided in a friend, and in his girlfriend, too. He wrote about it, and so can you when I give you his poetry back. It's a jigsaw that doesn't add up to a pretty picture."

"So you have the poems?"

"You can have them."

Her laugh was bitter. "How generous of you! Isn't that what I've been paying you for?"

"You'll get your poems," I said.

"Who the hell do you think you are, coming into my house -"

"Was Potts comforting you?"

"*What*?"

"Picking up the perks for being a shoulder to cry on? Or were you paying him to make sure that Simon got his First – so he could dedicate it to Terence?"

I felt the sudden sting of her hand as it slapped across my face.

"I've heard enough. Get out!"

"With his father dead and his girlfriend pregnant, he didn't even know what planet he was on. How were you paying Potts?"

"I said get out of my house!"

"Was it just money – or something even dirtier than that?"

"If you don't leave I will call the police."

"I'm going," I said. "But I've got something in the car for you. I hope those poems can tell you what you don't already know."

I took the poems from my glove compartment and walked back towards the house. She stood in the doorway, looking fragile and insignificant against the backdrop of that mansion.

But I was sick of being deceived.

I handed her the folders.

"Here," I said. "You've probably got copies already."

I went home and slept like the dead.

FIFTEEN

It was early and my phone was ringing. Carl was taking Angie to see Roy later and did I want picking up? I told him that I wanted some time to myself to mull a few things over. Carl kept asking if I was alright and I ended the call.

I went out to my car and told it that we had unfinished business in Leicester.

I sat in my car thinking, and I must have sat there for twenty minutes. Things were going back and forth in my head, in and out of focus. Finally I got out of the car and went back into my house. I rang Professor Potts.

I didn't expect him to pick up. When he did he sounded pleased to hear from me. But if he was expecting a social call he was soon disappointed. I told him that my friend almost died because he was out doing my job while I was chasing shadows.

Potts listened, and said all the right things, made all the right noises. I couldn't tell whether he was relieved or not when I said that I was calling it a day as far as the Hilary case was concerned.

He sounded like he was preparing to wish me all the best with the rest of my life, when I told him that I still had unfinished business in Leicester. I wouldn't say that he sounded particularly overjoyed when I announced that I needed to visit him one more time and preferably that day, Sunday or no Sunday. And if there was an undertone of unhappiness in his voice about the arrangement, he disguised it well enough, and gave me his home address. He said that he would be there all day.

I was about to end the call.

"Why did you join the police?" he asked me. "I never saw a person less suited to that occupation."

I asked what he meant by that, and he told me.

"The discipline, the formalities of the regime," he said. "It must have been a serious challenge for someone like you. But I have a theory, if you'd like to hear it."

He took my silence as a green light.

"I think you put on the uniform to protect you against the thug who put you in hospital."

"Protect me?" I said. "You don't think it raised the odds of me coming up against him?"

"Precisely," he said.

"You're confusing me."

"I doubt that very much. I think you understand me perfectly well. I think you've spent your life trying to confront your worst fears, and that's why you're coming back."

"Is that a fact?"

He was waiting for me to say something else.

I let him have it.

"My mother wrote stories. You know about that. She never wrote one about a student losing his father and standing to inherit a fortune. She never wrote about a student returning to university in the aftermath and finding a shoulder to cry on. Except that student chose a shoulder that inadvertently led him into dangerous waters, and to mix up my metaphors, turned him into the goose who lays the golden eggs. But people get too impatient and greedy and they put on too much pressure too quickly."

I listened into the silence for minute. Then I said, "You think Beth Hilary knows all this?"

"She would never admit it, Will, not even to herself. She would rather believe that God and the devil fought a

171

colossal battle over the life of her son, and that the devil won. *She* should have been the shoulder to cry on. And that's what's destroying her."

I'd left my car waiting long enough. I climbed in, pointed her down the hill, and set off back to Leicester.

*

Stephen Harris had the rest of Simon's poetry, though he claimed that he hadn't had chance to forward it on to me. If nothing else came of my journey back to Leicester, at least I was saving on postage.

I looked through the poems while Harris took a break from his studies and made some coffee.

There wasn't much to see; half a dozen works, some very short, and most of them abstract and difficult to follow. But one poem had a name contained in it. A name I didn't expect to find.

Paul.

Stephen Harris came back and asked if everything was okay. I showed him the poem and asked him about it.

"That was one of the last things Simon wrote, as far as I know," he said.

"Who's Paul?" I asked.

He shrugged. "I've no idea."

I read through the poem again. It seemed to be about a lover, though Sharon wasn't named. I didn't think it one of Simon's best poems. It seemed unfinished, and disjointed; at least a draft short of the finished thing, in my opinion. But then what did I know?

In the final lines Simon described a journey through a wasteland lined with ... *men looking for a war and Paul all dressed as Judas* ...

"Any idea what that's all about?" I said, and Harris confessed that he hadn't a clue.

"When Simon told you about going into town the night he met Sharon, did he mention anybody else?"

"No, only her."

"And nobody else visited you apart from Cartwright?"

"Nobody else, no."

"You said that Cartwright always came alone?"

"Both times, yes, that's right."

I took the poems and wished him well, the first of my goodbyes completed.

*

Ravenshill turned out to be a Scolders Rise for the risen, but hardly deserving of its name. There wasn't much of a climb, and I didn't see any birds that would have got Edgar Allen Poe excited. I turned into a neat little cul-de-sac and parked outside a detached property at the far end. If anything was to be gained here, tact and diplomacy was the order of the day.

Potts came to the front door before I'd got out of the car. He was smiling, looking pleased to see me.

"I'm so sorry about your colleague," he said as we entered his domain.

The house looked right for a professor. It had grandness about it but it was a long way short of homely. The little I saw of the interior suggested that every item could tell a story. But I wondered who there was in his life to tell those stories to.

He made coffee, and brought it through to a spacious lounge, where he gave me a lecture on the philosophy of communication. I wondered if he was trying it out for his undergraduates. My yawning didn't seem to make any difference to him.

"So what do you do when you're not solving mysteries?" he said at last.

"I read them."

173

"I love detective fiction," he said. "It must be the Wittgenstein within. I wish I had more of him, but, alas. I sometimes wonder what old Ludwig would make of our modern mysteries."

While he was wondering about what a dead Austrian philosopher would make of suicide in the Midlands in the twenty-first century, I wondered what the rest of the house was like. Everything but a bed was crowded into that room – sitting area, breakfast bar, endless racks of cassettes, CDs and records, a library of paperbacks and magazines, and a piano. I caught a flash of his life as lonely and full of empty imitation of what he thought a purposeful life ought to consist of.

When he disappeared to use the toilet I flicked through his CD collection. I was holding a copy of Scott Walker singing songs by Jacques Brel in my hand when he silently re-entered the room.

"Simon came here?" I said.

He nodded. "Yes, he did."

"You recorded a copy of this for him?"

"You're quite a detective. I don't know that music played a great part in Simon's life, but he was inquisitive about most things. I think he liked Brel's lyrics. He had taste."

"You wouldn't happen to like the *Now That's What I Call Music* series?" I said.

"That's a very odd question. Is it relevant?"

"Probably not."

I was imagining Simon putting on Brel for Sharon, and Sharon trying to offer something in return; and then perhaps Simon having the good grace to accept the gift.

"Why did you recommend me?" I said.

He rolled his eyes. "Not this again."

"What's your relationship with Beth Hilary?"

Twist

He looked at me hard, and while he was looking, I said, "And does the word blackmail mean anything to you?"

"Which would you like me to answer first?"

"Why was Simon here?"

"Simon came over for dinner once. We talked about philosophy. My indulgence was that I played the piano for him. But I sensed his boredom and put on Scott Walker to clear the atmosphere. Possibly the words intrigued him, though I suspect he asked for a copy by way of persuading me not to play any more piano. Sundays can be long and dull in Ravenshill. Simon brightened one, at least."

"You don't invite other students over?"

"I don't think the offer would be appreciated. Simon was a very special young man, and in many ways. He saw merits in the most unlikely places."

I wondered if he was referring to Sharon.

"Simon told you about Sharon Mackenzie."

"Simon confided in me."

"Why?"

"Do I have to explain everything?" he said, wearily.

"Maybe you do. When you recommended me, you recommended a third rate student, remember."

"You sound resentful."

"Do I? I can't begin to imagine why. You could have retrieved Simon's poetry yourself – it hardly required a detective."

He laughed.

"Have I said something funny?" I asked him.

"I think the penny's dropped," he said.

"Meaning?"

"There's more to this than finding a few poems."

"Then tell me what you're getting at, for God's sake!"

He placed his empty cup onto the coffee table in front of him and sat back in his chair.

"Like you," he said, "Simon lost his father."

"What's that got to do with anything?"

"Please, Will, if you will allow me to explain."

"Okay."

"I came to visit you in hospital. You were sleeping. I established that you would survive, and that you would return to your studies within a few days. You know about that; you even thanked me for the books that I left for you. But that experience changed you profoundly, I would say."

"What are you talking about?"

"The world was let in. I saw the same thing happen to Simon. You were two of a kind, detached from the world; full of curiosity about the world, yet not really a part of it. The books, and what we might loosely term 'reality' - the questions and the answers - they never matched up. Bereavement pierced Simon's bubble, and a thug pierced yours. It amounted to the same thing. Except that you survived."

He smiled, and I felt the warmth of it.

"When I came to visit you in hospital, I felt, well, like a father. Maybe you never saw it that way. But Simon, for a short time at least, did. He had to tell someone, and he couldn't talk to his mother."

"Why didn't you tell me this? What else haven't you told me?"

"I told Beth Hilary. I told her after Simon's death. That's how she knows."

The silence was full of questions. I was scratching the back of my head, and wondering, if I kept it up for long enough, whether a pile of sawdust would appear at my feet. I kept the thought to myself. After all, sarcasm was wasted on Professor Potts; he looked down on it all from too great a height.

"Let me tell you something," he said. "There are two kinds of fear: there's the fear that Mrs Hilary is experiencing, and the fear that you are going through. Beth Hilary is looking into hell. She is looking down into the abyss; into naked, nameless horror. For her the metaphysical universe is something vast and alive. It has to be, and do you know why?"

"Tell me."

"It contains all that's left of her family. All there is of Terence, and the resting place, and at the same time the playground, for her son, the love of her life, and its meaning."

"And what am I afraid of?"

"You're luckier than Beth Hilary. A mortal being can only gaze into the pit for the briefest moment, or else become a part of it. You want yourself back. You're not looking for anything out there – you're looking for William Twist. The young man who first came here, was looking for the boy who became lost in the disruptions of childhood. Personal identity is more than an essay title."

"Is that a fact?"

"You are what you do. This city treated you badly and it can do so again. You came back here to finish something. And I believe that you will."

"I'll never find the lowlife who put me in hospital, if that's what you mean."

"You don't need to."

I finished my drink, and all the time I never took my eyes off him. Physically he was a small man in a big room, but his words seemed to fill up all the spaces. He talked for a living and it was easy enough to fall under that kind of spell.

I blinked myself out of it. "That's some speech," I said.

"It was long overdue. Who said Freud was a good psychologist? Any man who tries to sum up the fears of the world by saying that boys want to kill their fathers and marry their mothers, is, and was, a profoundly sick individual. Freud may well have lain awake at night fearing the sound of scissors sharpening; I never did, personally. Use the ladder to climb up and see the world as it is, and then throw the ladder away."

"Wittgenstein?"

"I can't teach you anything. Plato said we can only recognise the truths within ourselves. Does that answer your question?"

"Not really," I said.

"That's a philosopher for you! Most of life is a shot in the dark, an act of sheer faith. I promised Beth Hilary nothing. We catch glimpses at best and sometimes we recognise truth. I happen to believe, yes, that there are huge metaphysical processes at work that are way out beyond our capacity to comprehend. The best we can do is observe, recognise the patterns, and resist the urge to extrapolate too much from too little. As a philosopher by nature as well as by profession, I like to think that caution is my hallmark. I also happen to believe that it might, on most occasions, be wiser to stick with the mundane explanation."

I watched him walk over to the piano. Time seemed to stop dead as he played. There was comfort in that.

Thoughts flew around my head, and I could see every one as a bird illuminated against the background of a clear, bright sky.

He was right: Beth Hilary had to believe there was more. That the decimation of her family lay at the centre of a cosmic battle between good and evil; it made sense when you framed it in those terms. She wanted a dreamer, a suggestible idiot; someone open to the possibilities.

And she got that. Professor Potts wouldn't conspire with her. He gave her me as a compromise.

As the music washed over and around me I saw a portal open up. I stood on the threshold.

He was telling me that there are two choices, two paths to take. You can walk through, find Simon, his life and death, knowing that Oldcastle has marked you as it marked him, and making you a part of a story as old as the world.

Or you can play out your part in the story as it was written for you: square up to evil manifest in the shape of the bully and lay your own ghosts to rest ... and in that sacrifice give Beth Hilary something sane to believe in.

I looked back from the threshold and asked him: "Is she mad?"

"That's for you to decide."

"Did she understand your rationale for recommending me?"

"At some level, yes, I believe so. But she likely could not articulate it and she will certainly never admit it."

The music stopped and I stood to go.

"Did Simon take his own life because of threats from Sharon MacKenzie's step-father - Todd Cartwright?"

I saw a look of disappointment register in his eyes. But I still didn't know what it meant.

*

I left his house and drove towards the estate, the sound of church bells calling the faithful. I wished I was one of them, wished I had a stronger framework to hold all my scattered and conflicting beliefs.

Something had changed, and whatever it was, whatever it amounted to, it brought with it a feeling of certainty.

That out of all the chaos and confusion of my life I was, at that moment, moving toward the right destination.

SIXTEEN

I pulled up along the street, a few doors from my original encounter with Sharon Mackenzie's charming family. The street was quiet, and I pictured a device buried just below the surface of the road, about to go off without warning.

During the drive from Ravenshill I couldn't shake the feeling that I was being followed.

My paranoia was getting out of hand. I decided to confront it, squaring up to it with logic; attempting to list the possible suspects: Potts tailing me to see if I got the last part of my job done; Beth Hilary following me from the very beginning – or else *having* me followed; checking if she was getting value for money; DI Sykes watching where I was poking my nose. *Todd Cartwright.*

It didn't look like Cartwright was home. I looked into the rear-view mirror, suddenly convinced that he was about to pull up behind me, having followed me all the way back from Potts' house to Oldcastle. He would be on to me by now; someone snooping around his daughter, asking questions about a student so shit-scared that he'd topped himself.

I checked the mirror again, and then I rang Sharon, and listened to a lot of abuse down the line. Cartwright was looking for me, and when he found me he was going to kill me.

I told her that was good because I was looking for Todd Cartwright and wanted to kill *him*.

"Anyway," I said, "enough of the pleasantries. What's Paul doing these days?"

"Paul?" she said.

"The friend to all skinheads. The one who led Simon to you in the French Revolution."

"What's he got to do with anything?"

"That," I said, "is precisely what I was wondering."

*

She was staying with a girl friend on the other side of the estate. She'd been living there since Simon died, having moved out of the family home. That's what she told me.

I followed her directions, arriving in a place less desolate than where Cartwright and Mother McKenzie were shacked up. It hardly felt like Oldcastle at all. The way the geography of the place had changed, maybe it wasn't.

I tapped on the front door, which opened in less than a second. She glared out at me, and I returned her look.

"So, you just use your folks' house for shagging students and detectives now?" I asked her.

"You can just fuck off if you prefer," she said.

"I'd rather come in. I'm not sure the neighbours need to hear this."

"They can fuck off too."

She let me in all the same, and we stood in the small kitchen.

"You want to meet Todd?" she said.

"That's right."

"Are you mental?"

"Quite likely I am. It has been suggested."

"He'll kill you – do you know that?"

"Why would he want to kill me?"

"Because he's a psycho."

"For no other reason?"

"How many reasons do you need? So why don't you go round and see him instead of coming here?"

"Did he have a nice time in Blackpool?"

She laughed. "Beer, chips and dog-fighting – that's his holiday. That's what a charmer that bastard is."

"You don't like him much, do you?"

"I wouldn't piss on him if he was on fire."

She eyed me for a moment. "What are you really doing here? Feeling horny?"

"Like I said, I'm interested in Paul."

"Why would you be interested in him?"

"Simon mentioned him."

"Who to?"

"In a poem, shortly before he died. Why do you think he would do that?"

"How should I know? You need a couple of glasses and a Ouija board, and then you can ask him yourself."

"Do you know where Paul lives?"

"I don't think that would be a good idea."

"Why not?" I asked.

The room fell silent and still.

Then I said, "When we hit town the other night, I thought I was asking the questions. But it was the other way around, wasn't it?"

"What are you talking about?"

"Do I make a good piggy-in-the-middle?"

"A good fucking loon-ball, more like. What are you on?"

"Is Paul involved in the blackmail?"

"What blackmail?"

"You know Simon's family are loaded. His death was no more than an inconvenience."

"What are you trying to say?"

"That it didn't stop the golden goose carrying on laying the golden eggs."

She came at me, fists and feet. It took all my strength to hold her off, and it was closer than I'm comfortable admitting, but there it is. My shins and ribs were stinging and aching, and one side of my face was throbbing, when her fury at last subsided and the tears came.

I gave it a few minutes, and then I started again.

"You're not aware that Todd or Paul or anyone else is blackmailing Simon's family?"

"Blackmailing them over what? That Simon knew a girl from the knicker factory, and that I was pregnant with his baby? That I loved him and he loved me? If there was anything else going on in that family, I didn't know about it. So how would Todd know, or anyone else round here?"

"So what's wrong with me going to see Paul?"

"Right," she said. "I've had enough of this. If it'll get you off my case, go and see him. I've got his address and his mobile. Which do you want?"

"Both," I said. "And I want you to come with me."

"I'm not going to tip him off, if that's what you're worried about."

I shook my head. "I'm worried about nothing of the kind. I just thought it was a nice afternoon for a romantic drive out."

In spite of herself she grinned. "The drugs must be good in Stone," she said. "Come on, then."

*

The feeling of being followed was haunting me. If anything it was intensifying, though I still couldn't spot a tail.

We were into a corner of the estate not exactly famous for its welcoming spirit, and not a million miles from Cartwright's stomping ground. Turning into a short street bordered on one side by untended playing fields beyond a rusting iron fence, Sharon told me to park up.

She pointed across the street.

"There. Nice, isn't it? The red door: number seventeen."

"You're not coming to say hello?"

"Somebody needs to stay behind and call an ambulance."

"Handy, is he?"

"Like I said, he knows people. Paul knows everybody. He might even know what the fuck you've been talking about."

I got out of the car.

"Sure you won't join me?"

She ignored my request. "Maybe *he's* blackmailing Simon's family," she said. "Why don't you go and find out, only don't come crying when it turns shitty and you get your legs broken."

"You almost sound like you care."

"Like you say: *almost.*"

*

A gaunt figure, with dyed black hair framing a face so white it might have been bleached, came to the door.

"Paul?" I said.

"Who's asking?"

"My name's Twist. I'm making enquiries into the death of Simon Hilary."

"Don't know anything about it."

His voice was lifeless; it suited his look.

"You're Paul?" I said.

"Where'd you get my name?"

"Can we go inside, please?"

"What do you want?"

"You met Simon."

"Did I? So what?"

"So I'd like to ask you some questions."

"Like I say, I don't know nothing."

I heard a car door close behind me. Sharon was walking towards us.

"How you doing, Paul?" she shouted.

"Shaz! What's all this about?"

We went inside the squat, into a room with boarded up windows, and sat in near darkness while I tried to find out why Simon had written the name 'Paul' into his last poem. If he smiled at Sharon once and asked her how Todd was doing, he must have done it a dozen times. We didn't stay long. There was no reason to. Sharon wished him all the best, and he said to make sure she told Todd to take good care of himself.

Back in the car, Sharon said, "Satisfied?"

"He doesn't sound like the Paul you described, with a legion of skinheads at his command."

"You saying I've taken you to see the wrong Paul?"

"Have you?"

"Don't be a dick. I only know one Paul and that's him. He's not been well. I think he's had some family problems."

"I think he's had more than family problems. Give me two minutes."

I went back to the house. This time Paul almost smiled, like I was an old friend he hadn't seen for a while; or at least someone who wasn't going to hurt him.

"What's Cartwright done to you?" I said.

"What's that?"

"Todd Cartwright. Why's he threatened you, why's he done this to you? What did you know about Simon Hilary? I can protect you from Cartwright. I can make it so that you don't ever have to worry about Todd Cartwright again."

His cold, dead eyes stared at me out of their sunken sockets.

"What do you know about blackmail, Paul? What about Roy Meredith – was it a warning?"

I could see no light of recognition in his eyes. "I don't know what you're talking about," he said.

"What about pornography? What about art dealers? Come on, Paul, you must have known about the shotgun wedding of the year …"

I hadn't realised that my hands were clutching at his shirt collar, until Sharon had hold of me and was yelling at me to let him go.

As she pulled me away, Paul was muttering, "I don't know anything, mate, honest, I don't know anything." Then he looked at Sharon and his eyes lit. "Hi, Shaz, how's it going? Tell Todd to take care of himself. Tell him from me."

*

We drove back to where Sharon was living. On the way she said, "Are you going to tell me what that was all about?"

"If I knew," I said, "I would tell you."

Maybe I was cracking up over Roy. Maybe I had no business here, digging into things that were making no sense, when I hadn't the facility left to count the fingers on my hands with any degree of certainty.

As we turned into the street where she was living, she said, "Todd's a mean twat but he's not stupid. He wouldn't waste his time warning people fifty miles away, he'd just come straight to you and break your head in or worse. And why would he hurt Paul? Drugs have done that already. You're not really much of a detective at all, are you?"

I pulled up outside the house. The feeling that I was being followed was getting stronger, and as we got out of the car I stood looking back the way we had come.

"Expecting anybody?" she asked. "My handsome stepfather? I tell you: you wouldn't last five seconds."

We went inside.

"Right," she said, as soon as the door closed. "You've seen Paul and he knows as much as I do: in other words, nothing. So if you think Todd knows more, you're going to have to ask him yourself. You know where he lives and you know what he looks like. But I doubt you've got the bottle, and even if you have, he's going to kill you anyway. Now, if there's nothing else ..."

Her mobile was ringing. It was playing the theme from some film that was dimly familiar, but I couldn't seem to nail it. Everything had become elusive.

"Hi, Mum. No, just chilling."

She looked at me.

"No, I don't think he'll be bothering me again."

She laughed at something. Then her expression changed, shot through with a sudden rage. "No, I've told you. I'll never live there again. I'll visit when that cunt's not there."

*

She hated Todd Cartwright as much as she'd loved Simon Hilary. The code of the estate: that you looked out for your own and cared for your own, no matter how they behaved or what they did – all of that was broken when it came to Sharon Mackenzie.

"Are you planning to visit Todd, then?" she asked me.

"What would it achieve?"

She sneered. "Some disappointment you turned out to be. That bastard wants putting behind bars for what he did, or putting six feet under. But no-one's got the stomach for it."

"Why don't you go to the police?"

"And tell them what?"

"Everything you know."

Her laughter sounded grim and hollow. "You don't know much about the real world, do you? It must be different in Stone."

She waited for me to respond. But I had nothing left to say.

"So will it stop now?" she said.

"Will what stop?"

"All these questions? Or will they keep sending people to try and prove that I must have been after something more than Simon?"

"I believe you," I said. "For what it's worth, I do."

I moved towards the door.

"I loved him," she said. "Maybe it never would've worked out because of who he was and who I am. We were too different. But I still loved him."

Then she said, "I was pregnant and I wanted his baby."

She saw the thought crossing my mind.

"And yes it was his and no, it wasn't like that. I didn't get pregnant on purpose. It was an accident. It was one of those things. But nobody believes that my sort get pregnant by accident. They think sluts like me know what they're doing."

"Did -"

"Did my mum know? *Todd*? That's the best part of all. They saw a chance for some serious money. That bastard was threatening Simon, telling him I was up the duff so he'd marry me or pay us off. He's never admitted it and Simon never said anything. But he wouldn't, would he?

He was the sort to keep his worries to himself. And look where it got him."

Her look became distant. "I got rid when he topped himself. Maybe I would have done anyway. Maybe Simon would have paid me off ... who the fuck knows how it would have worked out."

She laughed, and it was laughter filled to the brim with darkness. "I never told him I was pregnant. He knew though, and not because Todd told him. Simon wasn't stupid; he knew what that twat was all about."

She shook her head. "Todd had the scent, the scent of money. So he's out threatening Simon, no doubt, telling him he'd got me pregnant, and all the time I am – I was. But Todd doesn't fucking know it. There should be a word for something like that, for a mess like that."

"There is," I said. "*Irony.*"

"Fucking students!" she said, her laughter even more bitter now. "You're a clever bunch of bastards, aren't you?"

"And Simon never said anything?"

"I would have told him the next time I saw him. I never got the chance. But you know what? There was something bothering Simon – and I don't mean Todd Cartwright."

"What *do* you mean?"

"I don't know. He'd got exams, his dad dying, me for a girlfriend – I'm not saying it helped having that psycho throwing his weight around. But there was still something else. I never found out. Like I said, he was the sort who kept things bottled up."

I was trying to process it all, everything she had said, when a look came over her, and she moved towards me. "But it's all in the past now," she said. "Can't keep living in the past forever, can you. Got to move on – and you and me have some unfinished business."

Twist

I was rooted to the spot, uncertain of what was unfolding.

"I've got a reputation to think about," she said. "You finish what you started and then you get the fuck out of my life."

She was shedding clothes like loose change into a beggar's cup. I never heard the front door open.

But I did hear an old familiar voice screaming behind me.

"It's him again - I fucking knew it! Todd got a call off Paul. He's gone round there. I said I'd call here and Todd's on his way."

I looked at Sharon. But there was no sign of betrayal.

I barged past the old crone and through the door, fairly leaping into my car and pulling off, tyres screeching to highlight my whereabouts over a five mile radius.

*

After putting the miles between myself and the scene I pulled over at the edge of the estate. I thought about the dreams that I'd been having lately. About the weird stories telling my life, and how, in the final tale, my *not standing like a brave knight to battle the fire-breathing dragon* would result in the death and destruction of all I had known and loved.

Likely it had been prophecy all along, leading to this: that I had my chance to confront evil and had taken once again the coward's way.

Would this consign me to a lifetime of nightmare? I was certainly a deserving cause. I was sick of me. I was sick of thinking how all things related to *me*.

And so my thoughts turned back to where they ought to have been before this latest round of dereliction of duty.

Simon Hilary.

I saw him running, one grey Oldcastle dawn-come-twilight, flying with heels of fire across this filthy landscape … and … *at last I saw it.*

If Simon had ever run for his life from this place … where would he run *to*? Who could he confide in and who would give him shelter?

The blocks weren't safe. Stephen Harris' listening ear wasn't big enough or connected to a mind wise enough for the telling of this tale.

It was falling into place.

I drove back to Ravenshill.

SEVENTEEN

Professor Potts was about to leave his house when I arrived. I told him that I wouldn't take up much more of his time.

He led me through to his lounge. Noting my agitation, my "excitability", he asked if I had been drinking.

"Not today," I told him. "But I should have drunk more when I was doing philosophy. It clears the mind. Though not as much as seeing a friend smashed up and lying close to death in a hospital bed. I ought to be dead or at least in a coma by now, right?"

"What are you talking about?" asked Potts.

"The lamb to the slaughter," I said. "Being used; doing other people's dirty work. My part in this story ends with Todd Cartwright kicking the life out of me."

Potts started to speak; but I hadn't finished.

"I find out what's already known, and I shove my face in because of who I am and what I'm trying to confront, and Cartwright does the rest. True to form, he smashes that face to pieces, and goes to prison for killing me, or trying to. And everybody named Potts lives happily ever after."

The Professor didn't even blink. "What is it, what's troubling you?"

"I'll tell you what's troubling me. It has to do with what kind of comfort you were offering Simon in his hour of need."

"What are you suggesting, Will? What are you trying to say?"

"I'm not *trying* to say anything. I'm accusing you of taking advantage of a situation. Simon was frightened, grieving and desperate. He was being threatened by Cartwright, and he might have been trying to deal with blackmailers keen to fleece the vulnerable remains of his family. He had few places left to run and home wasn't one of them – it wasn't an option for Simon anymore, at least not as far as he was concerned."

His calm expression didn't budge. He waited for me to go on.

"And you knew all that, didn't you? And you offered him refuge, a bed for the night; shelter from the storm. But there's always a price, isn't there? There aren't many people in this world, in my experience, prepared to bail you out without it costing in some way. So, how's that for philosophical deduction, *Professor?*"

His calm expression held for a few moments longer, and then he stood up. "I think that you had better go now."

"I haven't finished."

"What do you want?"

"*The truth.*"

"Okay," he said. But he remained standing.

It was to be his final lecture.

"I recommended you for your compassion, and your understanding," he said. "That much remains true. And I never intended you harm, you must believe that."

"Must I?" I said. "Why? I think you wanted someone who wouldn't look too hard at you. You came to visit me in hospital, you showed me kindness and you're trading on that now. Beth Hilary wanted an investigation, and you wanted your own part in this kept hidden. So who better for the job than a failed policeman turned third-rate detective? Someone who owed you for a past kindness and a decent reference, but not the sharpest tool in the bag - isn't that the *truth*?"

He sat down, and I saw the resignation in his eyes. When he next spoke there were tears beginning to course down his crumpled cheeks.

"I never meant for you to get hurt, really I didn't. Simon came to me, desperate and frightened, as you say. And I gave him … the wrong kind of comfort. I've become a lonely old man, and I was very fond of Simon. I took my loneliness and his fear and grief and I betrayed the trust he had in me."

Hearing him say it, admit to it, I felt a part of the anger inside me starting to ease. Potts was already looking less the arch manipulator, and more the pathetic and lonely old man that he had just described. An empty shell of a man, with nothing left inside.

"There was loneliness at stake," he said, "that's all … loneliness and sanity. I exploited Simon, but not because of his family's wealth. It was never about money. Ironically, it was the other way around. Simon came to me that night *asking* for money, for a substantial sum of money."

"Did he say what he needed the money for?"

"He didn't."

"Why did he come to you?"

"Who else could he turn to? He couldn't ask his mother."

"Do you think the money was to pay Todd Cartwright?"

"I really don't know."

I didn't believe him. I pressed, my anger returning. "Was the money to make the threat of Cartwright go away? Or was it to pay Cartwright to make a different threat go away?"

He shook his head. "I don't know. But it struck me then, as it does now ... the 'coincidence' of his father's business partner dying the same day Simon died."

"But you gave him the money?"

"I did."

"And you know how that looks?"

"That I paid Simon ... like a cheap prostitute."

"Maybe not so cheap."

"That isn't funny."

"No," I said. "It isn't."

The silence grew and at last I stood up.

Who else was the money for but Cartwright? He couldn't go to his mother because she would want to know things that Simon couldn't tell her. So he came here, to Ravenshill, and satisfied a lonely old man to pay off an animal like Cartwright.

I left without saying goodbye.

EIGHTEEN

The sound of bells receded as I drove into the heart of the estate. In their place was the now constant, gnawing feeling that I was being followed. But if Cartwright was following me, what difference did it make? I had an appointment with him, one way or another.

I parked outside the house that Sharon had shared with her mother and step-father before Simon's death had forced her out. As I climbed out of the car clarity chose that moment to ambush me. It felt like a rock against the side of my head. I had not known such piercing illumination of the mind's cloudy eye since …

The truth was I had never known it.

I stood at the front door and knocked boldly. Oldcastle had become a single wooden door, a thin timber portal to a shrunken giant's castle.

I heard the footsteps approaching and saw the shadow loom through the patterned glass arch. I felt the impulse slip, the mind once again cloud into apprehension and confusion, leaving nothing behind save the urge to turn around and run and never stop running.

The door opened on Sheila MacKenzie. She was smoking something that looked like a cigarette but smelt like my old university days.

"What the fuck do *you* want?"

She took a step forward, and for a second it looked like she was going to fall off the step. Taking a moment to steady herself, she puffed heartily on the lighted stick in her hand. "My Sharon has been through enough, do you hear me!"

"Is she in?" I asked.

"So what if she is – what's that got to do with you?"

I tried to ask, politely, sensitively, whether I might have a quiet and civilised - even *private* - word with her daughter.

"Were you raised in a fucking orphanage – well, were you? When that girl's father fucked off, what was I supposed to do, eh? And don't give me any of that bull – so what do you want with my Sharon?"

She took another blow on the fire stick.

"Actually," I said, "I've come to talk to Todd."

"Ha, that's a coincidence! *He wants to talk to you.*"

"Happy days," I said. "Well, here I am."

She appeared confused. "Todd sees people when *he's* ready. You'll have to wait for him to find you. But when he does find you, you'll wish he hadn't."

"Can I speak to Sharon, then?"

"She doesn't live here anymore, you dumb shit! She just brings students and busy bodies here and fucks them when she thinks nobody's looking."

A familiar face appeared over Mother MacKenzie's shoulder as the matriarch stooped to cough deep and long in the narrow doorway.

"What do you want?" she said.

"Can we talk somewhere private?"

"You've got five minutes. Mum, let him through. He won't be staying."

The elder woman continued to gasp for breath as Sharon led me upstairs to her room.

It was like old times, but even more surreal without the anchor of a skin-full of booze inside me.

She sat on the bed. "Five minutes, and that's your lot."

"Sharon, listen -"

"I mean it, five minutes, so waste it how you like. You've got some nerve coming here. Some balls too, I'll grant you that. I never would have thought you had it in you."

"I've come to ask a favour."

"That's a good one. I've heard it all now. Are you saying I owe you or something?"

"It's about Simon."

"Can't you leave it alone? What can I do about that now?"

"There is something you can do," I said. "There's something that you can do for Simon."

Her hard expression softened and assumed a questioning hunger. Her fragility, her humanity, her need was suddenly quite beautiful, and my envy for what Simon once had stirred within me.

"You said he loved you."

The momentary softness vanished as quickly as it had arrived, to be replaced with a cast-iron glare. "Just who the fucking hell do you think you are?"

It was a fair question. Yet the persona I needed to get me through this was eluding me still.

"It's Cartwright you should be talking to," she said. "But I was right all along about you: when it comes right down to it, you haven't the bottle."

"I'm here, aren't I?"

"You watched him leave before you knocked, did you? You call that bottle? Waiting until the women are all alone? You're running out of time. You've got two minutes left."

I could see that she was still curious to hear what I had to say, otherwise I had no doubt that I would have been through the door, with her feet and fists employed to see me out.

"Shouldn't there be justice?" I said.

"For Todd Cartwright?" She sneered. "A bullet's the only justice a psycho like that understands."

The bedroom door burst open.

Sheila Mackenzie stood there, smoke still coming off her hand like a crazed gunfighter. "Come on, Shithead - out of this fucking house now!"

"He's going, Mum."

"He's bothering you. I can see he's bothering you."

"I can handle him."

"Oh, you can handle him! And if you can't, I can and Todd sure as fuck can."

"Leave us, Mum, will you!"

She pointed at me and gave me the death stare. "You do anything to harm my little girl and I'll fucking kill you."

Her cough retreated with her down the stairs.

"Look, Sharon," I said, "if you go to the police, they can put a case together. Extracting money with menace - you would be doing something for Simon -"

She cut me dead. "That's it? You come here and tell me I can *do something for Simon* when you know nothing apart from what I've told you. We've had this conversation once – and it's over, it's done with. Bastards like Todd Cartwright never get what's coming. The police couldn't give a shit. You get out of this house and you get out now."

She was heading for the door. "Mum!"

"Okay," I said, "I'm going." I grabbed her arm. "You were carrying Simon's baby. Doesn't that -"

The door flew wide, and the matriarch again stood seething. I could smell the whisky on her breath now as

200

she staggered into the room, falling onto the bed, clutching at her daughter. "Todd's on his way, Babe," she said, "Todd'll teach him, Todd'll do him proper."

I looked back to see the two women holding each other.

"If you change your mind, Sharon …"

"I won't - now fuck off out of here."

"You fucking heard her!"

I headed down the stairs and opened the front door to see Todd Cartwright charging down the front path.

In the time it took to get my breath he had me pinned against the door.

"What you doing in my fucking house upsetting my fucking family?"

"I -"

Words failed me.

"Lost your fucking tongue, Dickhead? Not so easy giving your shit to a man? Rather play it heavy with my wife and fucking daughter. I know all about you, nosing in other people's business."

My head was pressed hard against the door. I was surrounded by the stale smell of cigarettes and beer, the sound of coughing descending the stairs. "Smack the bastard one, Babes."

Cartwright's face was in mine, and all I could see were two dark eyes bearing down on me like shotgun barrels.

"So, what are you doing in my house?"

"I came to see Sharon."

"The wife says you was here the other night, while we were away. Fucking my daughter in my house – I could cut your balls off for that and nobody would argue the toss. So why're you back in my house?"

My power of speech was returning. I said, "I thought it was time we met, face to face."

"Are you trying to be clever? I'll cut your fucking tongue out."

No tongue and no balls. It wasn't an image to joke about.

Sheila MacKenzie was shouting about her poor girl, the orphanage days and the need for bloodshed.

The scene was like a bad-tempered reject from the *Twilight Zone* and I wondered if I had passed the point of danger and was going to end up invited for a traditional Sunday tea of salmon and cucumber sandwiches.

He let go of me and turned on his wife, telling her to shut her stupid mouth and to get back inside the house. Then he turned back to me, giving me my first opportunity to really take a look at the man in the full splendour of his ugliness.

It was a magnificent sight, in its own way. He looked every inch the boxer who had gone to seed but who would still know all the tricks and how to break somebody's face open with a couple of slaps.

My handful of Kung Fu sessions decades ago seemed as useful now as they had been to the poor student who had walked into the wrong place at the wrong time and wasted two careers trying to put the mistake right.

"You want to see Sharon but she doesn't want to see you - you know what that makes you, Dickhead? It makes you a fucking dickhead, Dickhead."

I thought about asking him if he had ever thought of studying advanced logic for brainless bastards.

"I asked you a question, Dickhead."

"I'm here because of what you did to Simon Hilary."

"Never heard of him."

"Sharon was pregnant with his child."

His eyes glowed like pigs on fire.

"Did Paul ask too many questions? Did he know more than was good for him? Did he open his mouth too wide and too often?"

His look of disbelief was a picture, but not one that I wanted mounted above my bed.

A fist buried itself inside my guts and tore the breath from my body. I doubled over.

"Oops," he said. "That was clumsy of me. I was reaching to get the hanky out of my trousers."

I straightened up. His blow felt heavy, but it had missed the solar-plexus and all the other sacred regions. I made it look worse than it was. As a child I excelled at playing dead. I could have won awards for some of those performances. I began to wonder, with dim hope, if this man's fighting days were longer past than I'd imagined. My anger was stoking my bravado now, and in the end I went for it.

"Come on," I said. "You must remember Simon Hilary? You paid him a couple of visits, making secret arrangements for a fairy tale wedding." I winked at him. "Loaded, he was. You could have been nicely set up there if you'd played it a little more like a human being and less like a shit-for-brains-animal."

I could feel the years bumping off each other in hateful collision. Every day I wore the uniform dreading this confrontation. The beating up of a student; the schoolyard scraps and the threats issued in cloakrooms that never amounted to anything but which, in their sworn-on-the-Bible promise, had led finally to this day of days; this lost and abandoned moment in time when all the paths of my life crossed and stood in awe of what mighty thing was coming to pass.

Here I was.

Alive.

"Who are you? And don't say the fucking police …"

"Not anymore," I said.

"Not some bent arsed investigator?"

I was clinging to the wild notion that looking away, showing weakness, would sign my death warrant. On this rationale, and this alone, I looked the ugly bastard straight in the eye and said, "Simon Hilary took his own life because of you."

He laughed. "Little twat couldn't handle the pressure. Don't need wimps like that round here."

"His father died and then he met your daughter, fell in love, and you saw the chance to earn a few quid."

"Love! He shagged her, the dirty bastard. But don't come here talking to me about love."

"You shouldn't judge everybody by your own high standards."

"You what?"

"Or maybe it wasn't suicide after all. Where were you the night Simon Hilary died?"

"And what night would that be?"

A savage light flashed into his eyes. "Oh, it's coming back to me now. I was at a party at The Spirit. An all nighter it was and I was there for all of it. Whatever night you're talking about, I was there. So tell me - how many witnesses do you need?"

"You surprise me," I said.

He frowned.

"Hiring others to do your dirty work?"

"I do my own, always have done." He spat in my face, and I felt the slime trickling down my cheek. "You know nothing!"

Sharon came to the door. "Todd, I can handle this." She looked at me with hate and pity. "Go, will you, just fuck off."

I turned back to Todd Cartwright. "She loved him, do you know that?"

"Leave it, will you," she said. "Just go."

"Tell him, Sharon. You could have made it up about the baby - but you didn't. Tell him!"

"Tell me what?" said Cartwright.

"Tell him you were pregnant."

"What's he fucking talking about?" said Cartwright.

"Not just the scam pregnancy that excuse for a mother dreamed up. Tell him about the real thing, flesh and blood."

"You think he cares?"

She was shaking. I wondered how many levels of fear were operating to keep her from flying the wretched nest once and for all. That excuse for a home, the factory. *Oldcastle.*

I looked back into the eyes of the beer dragon, and felt my earlier clarity return like the ghost of a warrior who had existed only in dreams. I had the notion to tell Cartwright some truths while I lay dying with the dignity of having my hand in the shape of a fist.

"You're as ugly as the life you lead, Cartwright. You're a blot on the landscape of civilisation."

His mind was struggling to make sense of the word shapes coming out of my mouth.

I watched his glorious confusion: what was a cornered animal like me – a skin and bone detective – doing talking to the mighty Godfather Todd Cartwright with such lack of respect?

"The likes of you tried to snuff me out twenty years ago, but you got Simon instead. Like him I strayed out of the paddling pool and into the open water where sharks like you feed."

He was thrown out of kilter by my strange death bed speech, his eyeballs spinning as his half-dozen brain cells struggled to compute what was going on.

"You were the wolf who chased Simon Hilary out of the bed of your daughter and into the arms of a leper."

He was painting the targets on my face and body. Then I watched him turn away, looking at Sharon. "What is this stupid twat talking about?" he asked her.

"I'm talking about the blood of Simon Hilary on your hands and the blood of the baby your step-daughter was carrying – and that's also on your hands. And I'm talking about how you screwed up the one great chance of happiness in her life because you're a greedy, vicious lump of nothing who terrifies, or tries to terrify the world into not daring to tell you what's right under your nose."

He'd heard all he needed to hear from me. All of his attentions were focused on Sharon. "Is this true? You were pregnant?"

"What do you care?"

"You stupid bitch! You stupid fucking bitch!"

I saw a tear forming in her eye in the instant before she screamed.

He went for her and I grabbed at him, my arm locked around his fat neck. Then the tables turned and something that was probably a fist swung down into my face and temporarily blinded me. I could hear more screaming, voices merging into one as the rain of blows started to come thick and fast and I felt myself going down. Martial arts moves, Grasshopper, Carradine – all had long ago deserted the stage, and I felt the loneliness at the core of William Twist. And when I could see again, I could see only blood.

Twist

From somewhere above the red deluge I thought I heard familiar voices in the seconds before the light faded and everything went black.

NINETEEN

It was Josie's birthday. I had a parcel, done up neatly in Disney wrapping paper and finished off with a bow. We were in an adventure park, the sun was shining, both of us worn out from the day. At a kiosk I ordered two lemonades and two ice-creams, and we took them over to a picnic table. Josie was telling me that this was the best birthday ever. She ate her ice-cream and half of mine, and her eyes were on the beautifully wrapped parcel.

I watched her carefully unwrapping the present, though I couldn't for the life of me remember what it was I'd bought, or from where. She peeled off the bow, placed it carefully on the table next to her lemonade, and sat looking at the package, savouring the anticipation. I thought she was going to start ripping at the paper but instead she took a long swig of her drink, smacking her lips for good measure.

What if she didn't like it?

Why couldn't I remember what I had bought my own daughter for her birthday?

The sun had disappeared behind a thick, black cloud while a cold wind was blowing up out of nowhere.

Suddenly we were in the middle of the estate …

… Someone standing over me …

… A voice, a woman's voice, calling me, but not making any sense … "*Where*?" I framed the word … it repeated on my lips …

… I felt the prick of a needle in my arm, and then I was off again, on another adventure …

Twist

I never found out what Josie was unwrapping.

*

Most of my dreams contained strange music and portals into other dimensions; stories written by a sick mother.

Professor Potts was telling me about an interview with her that he had found on the internet. She was thinking of writing a story where everybody dies. I was telling him she'd already written it: a tale about Oldcastle, the monster emerging from the shadows, devouring everything I loved.

I dreamed that the hospital was a dream, filled with spectral nurses and doctors using obscene drugs to keep me prisoner in a purgatory written for me by my mother. They were using hope to torture me: a day of discharge promised and looming.

Potts came, or I dreamed that he came, and I told him about my dreams.

All he said by way of reply was that an occult explanation for the death of Simon and Terence Hilary would have been a damn sight easier to swallow than an account of his "little Grasshopper" visiting the giant in his own forest and squaring up to him Hollywood style.

*

I woke up screaming, clutching at something. Behind closed eyes I had been transported back to Oldcastle to witness the destruction of everyone I had loved. One by one they were taken down into the pit, a vast and smoking crater that dominated the estate, feeding hungrily on friends, and on family, while the voice from the sky mocked my cowardice and ignorance as it prepared to take down my little girl.

Another voice was telling me it was okay: *I was only having a nightmare!*

*

Another blast of morphine arrived and I was off on my travels again. This time I was back in the pages of the book of my life. I knew that it was marked as the final visit, and that everything would be determined and fulfilled.

And I was filled with blinding amazement. A miracle had occurred.

Everything had changed.

The detective had not run away as the estate buckled and crumbled behind him, finally catching and destroying him. He'd stood his ground, and when the giant smoking pit opened up, it took down only the monster.

In the final pages of the book, in the last story of all, the triumph of evil had been mysteriously replaced by something smelling suspiciously of redemption.

... and as the edifice shook and the entire structure collapsed as dramatically and symbolically as the one described by Poe, the cracks widened in all directions like exposed veins brimming with black blood, every brick crumbling until the main arteries themselves became choked. And the detective knew that the first battle had been won: that the dragons of the past had been slain, giving him the faith and power to confront those of the present and one day the future. Tonight he would sleep in the company of dreams that promised nothing but enlightenment and reconciliation and always, always *love ...*

*

Angie brought flowers and a kiss. The combination almost broke my heart. The days passed and the dreams and visits thinned, but clarity was returning. Carl visited and I asked what had kept him. I found out later that he

210

had spent the first three nights at my bedside, subsequently splitting his time between Roy and me.

"Any change with Roy?" I asked him.

"That's the first good news of the day," he said. "It looks like he's going to make it."

I let the news sink in, the joy and relief of it flooding through me. Then I asked him, "What's the other good news?"

"They're holding Cartwright."

"His fishing licence expired?"

"Attempted murder."

"Who's he attempted to kill?"

"You, you fool!"

"There's never a black belt around when you need one."

He looked away a little too quickly.

"Carl?" I said.

I recalled the grim moments at Cartwright's Castle as I went down, the familiar voices, the earlier sense of being followed. I saw too the marks around Carl's eyes when he removed his sunglasses.

"You ...?"

He was shaking his head. "I can't take too much credit. It's DI Sykes you should be thanking. That man can fight."

"*Sykes*?"

"He was following you for days, apparently."

"What were you doing there?" I asked Carl.

"You were acting a bit strange," he said. "I was worried about you. And then Angie asked me to keep an eye on you and I took it to heart. When you told me you wanted some time alone, I thought: that boy's not telling his Uncle Carl what's really on his mind. So I thought I'd take a look at what was so interesting in Leicester. I thought I'd got you taped when I saw the girl; she could warm a winter night and leave plenty over for spring. Anyway, Sykes clocked me following you, except I rumbled him and switched it around so that for a while I was following him."

"It sounds like the Keystone cops," I said.

"I collared him on the estate. Or maybe he collared me – it doesn't really matter. But you've got two good witnesses to say that Cartwright was planning to rip your head off."

"It feels like he made a half-decent job of it."

"You'll survive. And you managed to break a bone in his fist, too."

"What happened to all that karate?"

"Cartwright's never heard the rules. If it wasn't for Sykes it would have been a double murder. When they finally took Cartwright away there were four patrol cars. But the work had already been done. Sykes loved every minute."

I asked if Carol, my ex, had been informed and he answered with a nod of his head.

"That interested was she?" I said. "How's Josie?"

"Carol didn't say much about anything."

I shouldn't have been surprised.

As Carl stood up to go, I said, "The police would never have got to me fast enough. In Oldcastle they let them kill each other and send a cart around to pick up the bones in the morning. Thanks."

After he'd gone I noticed something hiding on my bedside table, behind the orange cordial and the biscuits. Somebody had brought in my photo of Josie and had it properly framed.

That's when something wet and largely unfamiliar started rolling down my face.

Twist

I was dozing on and off when I heard another voice. It sounded like Potts, and at first I thought I was dreaming. He was telling me about the night that Simon stayed at his house in Ravenshill, and at some point I realised that I wasn't dreaming at all. But I still kept my eyes closed.

I don't think, looking back, that I fooled him for a second. He knew I wasn't asleep.

"… Here we are again, Will ... twenty years on and back at your bedside ... don't think badly of Beth Hilary, she would not have done anything to hurt her son, not for the world … everything she did was to protect him … she may have tried too hard, who's to say? ... I tried to help, I tried to be something ... something I could never be … I tried to take the place of a beloved father, to be a listener … I could never give up trying to be the wise counsellor ... for Simon ... for Beth … I didn't recommend you because I thought you were a fool ... I wanted somebody to help her ... someone who would understand not as a policeman understands but as a victim … as you were once, lying here all those years ago … I'm a lonely old man and Simon needed someone to talk to ... to help bear his secrets … I was fond of him and then I thought too much of him and tried to be too many things to him ... and I went too far and yes that night that one night I invited him into my bed and we lay there together in the warmth ... protecting him ... no, protecting each other ... against the cold and hostile world outside ... and all we did was cry and hold each other and cry and cry … and I have resigned my post at the University this morning … and I will regret every day for the rest of my life because I will never know what in the end drove Simon to that final act of desperation … I will never know … I will never know for sure that it was not me …"

*

I was getting ready to leave the hospital when Sykes turned up. He seemed different, like I was seeing him for the first time. I'm not saying he was about to vote for me as detective of the year, but I got the impression that I had gone up a notch from being the dirt beneath his shoes. Maybe he just wanted something that he thought I could give him.

He wasted no time getting down to business.

"I hear you're off back to Stone," he said. "Do you have any plans to visit Beth Hilary?"

Before I had chance to answer, he said, "I think you should. Call in at the station and I'll bring you up to date."

"You think she organised the hit on Ralph Sterling?"

"Frankly I think that's highly unlikely. But like I told you before, I'm not really interested in who killed Sterling. I am interested in why Sterling was blackmailing Beth Hilary."

And with that he was gone.

TWENTY

When Carl came to take me home I asked if we could call on Roy. And when Roy saw me standing at the end of his bed in my hero's slings and bandages, it was all he could do not to laugh.

"You ought to see the other guy, Roy."

"You ought to see the other guy, Will."

They were planning to move him out to an orthopaedic hospital, though it was too soon to know if there would be life outside of a wheelchair for him. With the three of us in that side ward it was like DMT reformed and I wondered if there was still hope.

He wanted to know about the case and I told him. When I'd finished updating him, he said, "An interesting final case for DMT."

I glanced at Carl and then I looked back at Roy.

"It's the end of the road I'm afraid," he said, "for me at least. I'm hanging up my detective shoes. It's about time. But there's nothing to stop you and Carl ..."

He smiled, and it was a smile tinged with sadness. "I'm looking forward to my retirement. It's the start of a new chapter and I'm quite excited. Anyway, I still want to know how this case turns out. Sykes is like a dog with a bone – he must hold you in high regard to follow you around and ask you to go back to see Mrs Hilary."

"I don't see why he thinks I can get any more out of her than he can."

"That's your low self esteem talking," said Roy. "I think it's time you gave yourself a break."

215

"Spoken like a Stone philosopher," said Carl, and the three of us laughed.

*

The next day I went to the office. Carl had started winding things down. The money from Beth Hilary had seemed like a lifeline a few days earlier, but appeared all but insignificant now.

I rang DI Sykes, and he answered on the first ring. I was halfway through thanking him again for his timely intervention in saving my life, when he cut me short. "Do you need a car sending or are you making your own way here?"

*

It was the first time I'd set foot in a police station since leaving the force in Leicester. I didn't exactly feel at home, not even when Sykes thrust a plastic cup of something hot and sludge-like into my hand and told me to sit down.

"Cartwright bought himself a Range Rover recently," he said, "a brand spanking new one at that. All the extras, top of the range. It's raising a few questions like: how did an arsehole like that stretch his benefits to pay for it - cash!"

I tried a sip from the steaming cup before placing it on the table next to me. Sykes took a mouthful from his own cup and swallowed it down without flinching.

"We followed the line that he'd been extracting money with menace from Simon Hilary. That this had led directly to Hilary taking his own life."

Sykes took another mouthful, draining the scalding liquid from the plastic cup.

"He denied it, of course. So we asked where the money had come from. He said it came from Simon Hilary but that it was given willingly. Cartwright reckons he was approached by Hilary to hit Ralph Sterling. To have Sterling killed."

"Cartwright would say anything to save his neck."

Sykes looked at me as though I had committed some grave sin. "Is something wrong with my coffee?"

"I'm sorry," I said. "I'm not thirsty."

He didn't look convinced.

"Okay," he said. "This is how it is. Cartwright's suggesting Simon Hilary paid him up front. Being a dumb student who knew nothing about the ways of the world, and imagining that enough money in the bank could solve just about anything, he handed the cash over and expected a result. Cartwright thought it hilarious. He assured Hilary that everything would be taken care of and then pocketed the cash with no intention of doing anything. And why should he? The money was in his pocket and what could Simon Hilary do about that? Go to the police? Demand the money back?"

Sykes waited for my response.

It was stupid enough to be true. Simon would have been roughly an ocean out of his depth dealing with the likes of Todd Cartwright, and desperate enough. The whole thing had a ring of hideous credibility. It gave Cartwright a way out of the extorting-money-with-menace rap, so long as Simon had a reason to want Ralph Sterling dead.

And that's where I came in.

" ... You believe Sterling was blackmailing Beth Hilary?" I asked him.

"I think there's a strong possibility."

"You don't think he could have been blackmailing Simon?"

"That doesn't work for me."

"Even though Simon borrowed money and tried to organise the hit?"

"Blackmailing Simon over what? Where's the angle? I think he was trying to help his mother."

I told Sykes what I'd gleaned from Stephen Harris: about Simon overhearing his father's conversation on the phone – or one side of it. Terence Hilary had been afraid of something, and Harris suspected blackmail because Simon's parents were wealthy.

Sykes listened intently and nodded. "It makes sense. But if Sterling was blackmailing Terence, and then switched to blackmailing Beth after her husband died ... I want to know the angle."

"Fair enough," I said. "But why do you imagine I could make a better job of finding out than you?"

He grinned. "Have you looked in the mirror?"

I wasn't altogether sure what point he was trying to make.

"You look like a hero returning from battle," he said. "And I reckon she's a sucker for someone with your kind of injuries."

With a delivery as dry as the one DI Sykes was employing it was difficult to tell if he was being serious.

I said, "Sterling was Terence Hilary's business partner. By all accounts he didn't have many scruples. But is it credible he could get away with blackmailing Terence Hilary, and then Beth Hilary, when that would run the risk of exposing his own shady dealings?"

"That depends what he was blackmailing them over, doesn't it?"

I still wasn't sure what he was suggesting, though I had my growing suspicions. I chose not to voice them, and Sykes wasn't saying anything.

"Any more questions?" he said.

"If Cartwright pocketed the money and did nothing, what happens to Cartwright?"

Sykes shrugged. He was good at shrugging. "Who cares? That's for the Leicester mob to sort out."

I was at the point of raising again the question of who killed Sterling.

"Before you ask – that's for the London lot to sort out. It probably has nothing to do with any of this. I'm interested in Beth Hilary. I want to know why Sterling was blackmailing her."

"But if Sterling was blackmailing her, wouldn't it at least be a possibility that she was involved in setting up the hit?"

"It might," he said, looking not the slightest bit interested in the possibility. He pointed at my coffee. "You're not drinking that, then?"

He leaned forward, looked into the murky depths, lifted the plastic cup and poured the remains of its contents down his throat.

"Good luck," he said.

TWENTY ONE

I still wasn't driving and so I took a taxi to West Hampton to see Beth Hilary one last time. In the back of the cab I closed my eyes and thought of Simon. I wondered where his final resting place was. I was certain he had been buried and I dimly recalled there being a church service.

As we approached West Hampton I asked the taxi driver where the nearest church was. He thought for a moment. I said, "Do you go to church?"

He was a fifty-something African with a face full of scars and history. He shook his head. "I should do, but I don't. This job gives me no time for nothing. But I got dependants to think about, so there it is. I think the church you're looking for is St Paul's."

He took me there and I asked him to wait. He said the meter would be running, church or no church. I said, in my moment of abandon, that I didn't care whether the meter ticked all night.

It was dusking over but the sky was clear, with a bright moon lighting the churchyard behind the small gothic church. At the far side of the graveyard I could see where the fresher burial ground had been opened up to make room for the latest additions to the growing population of the dead. It didn't take me long to find the gravestone.

There was nothing ostentatious about the gravesite. A small stone with simple words inscribed; a scattering of flowers, a few cards and messages. I had a feeling that Sharon Mackenzie would visit this place if she hadn't already.

There was a small photograph of Simon. He was smiling, appearing bright and unafraid; a young man with the world waiting for him. A version of life before everything clouded over.

It occurred to me that if my mother had been writing Simon Hilary's story, her love of dark irony would have meant only one possible outcome: Beth Hilary would have been the orchestrator of her son's doom, albeit inadvertently. She would have organised the hit on Ralph Sterling, and when Simon heard of Sterling's death, guilt would have done the rest. It would in its own way have been perfect.

And yet DI Sykes wasn't having any of it.

Why?

Because Sykes had another theory – and every bit as dark.

I looked up at the sky and saw the stars appearing one by one as the day dimmed around me. Then I turned from the graveside and walked back towards the church.

Passing the arched entrance, I had an urge to go inside. I walked up to the door and tried the handle. But the door was locked.

I got back into the taxi, and as we headed up the road, I noticed the tail of the car in front as we turned off back towards town. I was certain that it was Beth Hilary's car.

"While I was in the churchyard, did any cars stop outside?"

"Just one," said the driver. "It was nice, too."

"A Mercedes convertible?"

"Yes, that's right. A woman with dark hair got out and walked as far as the church, and then she came back to her car." He turned and winked at me. "Don't worry," he said. "I can be discreet."

When he dropped me off at the end of Beth Hilary's drive he winked at me again.

"You want to get that seen to," I told him.

"What's that?"

"You've got something dirty in your eyes."

*

Beth Hilary answered the door like she was expecting me. She made a fuss about how I looked and was I alright, and then she invited me inside. The last time we parted we had hardly been the best of friends, yet anybody watching would never have guessed it. Perhaps Sykes was right all along: my battle scars working my ticket.

As we walked through to the living room I noticed that most of the paintings had gone. The walls were almost bare.

"I've been tidying up," she said. "The last house that needs a curse is this one."

I couldn't argue with that.

"I never meant for you to get hurt," she said.

"There's nothing that won't mend," I said. "Don't worry about it."

She smiled; a candle lighting up the gloom.

I said, "I believe our mutual friend has resigned his post at the university."

"You know, then? About ..."

"The question is: how much do *you* know?"

She offered to make a drink. I declined her offer. Then she invited me to sit down, before taking her place opposite.

She was looking older, and had lost weight that, it seemed to me, she could ill afford to lose. It showed in her face; the bones too prominent, the skull revealing itself beneath the skin.

"I don't blame him," she said. "He's not why Simon took his own life."

"You accept that your son committed suicide?"

"It was all there in the poems, everything, even the baby. Some of it's hiding between the lines, most of it, in fact; but it's there."

"You didn't need a private detective after all – just a literature student."

"A mother knows when her son is in love."

She looked at me, as though trying to make her mind up about something. Then she looked away, a sorrowful look engulfing her.

"And a mother knows when her son is holding onto a secret so shameful that …"

She stopped, her eyes burning into me. I wasn't altogether certain what she was looking for.

I said, "Are you talking about Potts – or do you think it's shameful that Simon was in love with a girl from the estate ... a girl who sewed underwear for a living?"

"What do you take me for?"

I didn't answer.

"You think me a terrible snob, don't you?"

"You're no worse than I am," I said.

"You don't mean that."

"Oh, I mean it," I said, "believe me. If I've learnt nothing else these past days ... but that's another story. I'm intrigued though: if it wasn't the gulf in social standing, what was so shameful? Simon getting somebody pregnant before he'd finished his education?"

"Damn you!" she said.

"Professor Potts? Did he tell you everything?"

"That depends on what you mean by everything, doesn't it? I know that he abused his position of trust, if that's what you mean. I know that Simon went to him out of desperation and that he …"

She broke off.

When she started talking again, her tone was lighter. She said, "I saw the changes in Simon, despite the grief over his dad. I didn't know this girl, except through my son. But if he thought so much about her, she couldn't have been a bad person."

"You've met her?"

"I met her at the hospital, at your bedside. If things had worked out differently, of course I would have tried to talk Simon into seeing *sense*."

She laughed, scornfully.

"Like I'm the relationship guru in this family! I couldn't easily have embraced this girl as my daughter, being what I am. But that was then. So much has happened. Things have changed. None of us are the people we were."

"What about the baby?"

"My grandchild? What do you think? Do you think it would have been right of me to expect her to raise a child to keep a grandparent happy? And had she done so, would I or anybody else have been capable of *not* questioning her motives? I don't blame her for what she did. It's all part of the tragedy."

"Did Simon ask you for money, a substantial sum of money?"

She shook her head. "Potts gave him the money."

"Do you know why Simon needed the money? Do you know what he intended to do with it?"

She didn't appear to recognise the question.

I thought of what Sykes might have been implying when he sent me on this errand; when he appeared to rule out Beth Hilary being involved in the murder of Ralph Sterling.

But I still had to clear it out of the way.

I said, "Simon asked you for money, and you thought he wanted it to pay Sterling off, didn't you? Was Sterling getting greedy, coming to Simon as well; or did your son find out about the blackmail? You used some of the contacts you'd made through Terence, with his shady business dealings, and you decided to deal with Ralph Sterling once and for all ..."

She was on her feet. "For God's sake, man – you don't have the first clue what you're talking about. I don't know those kinds of people and neither did Terence, like I told you before."

She was cracking.

"Except ... oh, my God, why did he have to do it? Wasn't I enough for him?"

The pain was raw, glimpses of it screaming out through her eyes, the weight of it crushing her. She collapsed back into her chair.

"We'd been so happy for so long. I knew there was something going on. He wouldn't admit it, but I knew him too well, for too long. When he came back from London the last time ... I confronted him and he told me. We went out walking. He told me he was leaving me. How could I bear it? What would I do? And Simon ... how would that affect my son? He was studying so hard ... his finals coming up ... the timing ..."

"You killed Terence?"

"I didn't plan to. But I couldn't stand to see him turn his back on me. It happened before I even knew what I was doing. I didn't plan to ... and when it was done ... I couldn't face the thought of what the scandal would do to Simon."

"And Ralph Sterling knew?"

"Ralph Sterling was blackmailing Terence when he found out about my husband's affair. He knew what I'd done, and he gave me the choice: he would go to the police or I would pay the price another way."

"And you chose to let him blackmail you?"

"I did it first for Simon. But when Simon was gone I had nothing left. I hired you to tell me the rest of the story of my son's life. But maybe I hoped that it might lead you to the truth of what I've done."

"Do you know that Simon paid for Ralph Sterling to be killed?"

She looked at me, lost in her grief. Slowly she fixed her eyes on mine and nodded. "He took his life later the same day that Sterling was killed. He couldn't live with it. What other conclusion is there?"

I had to give her something. I said, "Simon may have paid for that, but he was not responsible for the killing of Ralph Sterling."

She looked dazed. I didn't know how much she was hearing now; how much she was taking in.

"Cartwright took your son's money. But he had no intention of using a penny of it to have Sterling killed. He bought himself a car with that money. Simon was too naïve, too good, too innocent to know how to move in the world of lowlifes like Cartwright and Sterling. Your son has no blood on his hands. It's a measure of the man he was that he had to kill himself out of guilt for something that he didn't do."

She came out of her trance. "You're saying that my son died for nothing?"

She stood up. "The secret, the shame that Simon was bearing, was that I, his own mother, killed his father, the father he loved so much. That was what drove my son to

226

take his own life, regardless of whatever the final trigger might have been. But I couldn't accept it. I wanted to find something else to believe in, someone else to blame. That's what you were doing here ... that's what I wanted you to find."

She was falling to pieces in front of me. I went to her and held her as the tears came down.

When at last she pulled away and wiped her face, she said, "Is DI Sykes waiting outside?"

I shook my head.

"Good. I have one more favour to ask. Will you go with me to the police station?"

"Of course," I said.

"Thank you. But first I have to leave my affairs in order. I want to make sure that Sharon is taken care of. She's thinking of going to college."

"You're not ..?"

"Paying her way? Why not? What else have I got to spend it on now? And anyway, I'm not going to be around. There's a price to be paid, and that's fine."

She smiled. "You met her mother?"

"She would have made an interesting in-law."

Our quiet laughter seemed desperate and jaded, but it was the best we could manage under the circumstances.

She went over to the desk and drawers that stood in the corner of the room, and wrote out a cheque, handing it to me. I told her that I couldn't possibly accept anything more than she'd paid already.

"You can possibly and you will. I'm sorry about your friend, your colleague, really I am. It'll buy you all some time."

It would do that. About three lifetime's worth.

"I have something else for you," she said. "You'll have to come upstairs to get it."

227

I followed her up the stairs, and stood in the doorway, watching her go into her bedroom.

The room was big, grandly decorated and furnished, but my eyes focused on the bed, which looked cold and empty.

She came back to the doorway holding something behind her back.

"There's a special child in this world, and in a few days she's going to be six years old. Her daddy loves her very much but he doesn't have the first clue how to show it. He spends so much time thinking of the perfect words, trying to find the perfect gift, and he ends up saying nothing and buying nothing."

She handed me an exquisitely wrapped parcel.

"What is it?" I asked.

"Well," she said, "you have two choices. You can open it, in which case you'll have to wrap it again – and I've yet to meet the man who could tie up a bow like this. Or you can develop a little faith."

She kissed me. "Thanks for everything."

I hesitated, looking down the landing towards Simon's room. I had one more question to ask her.

Recognising the dangers, but choosing to ignore them, I said, "Did Simon ever listen to *Now That's What I Call Music*?"

"I don't recall him being a fan. I wouldn't have thought that was Simon's cup of tea."

I said, "Do you mind if I take one last look?"

"Be my guest," she said.

We walked along the landing, and she followed me inside her son's room.

I went over to the chair with the collared white shirt still draped over it, and the Jacques Brel recording sandwiched between the book of Donne's poetry and the

Now CD. Time standing still - or was it? Had something lifted?

"Do you mind if I ..?"

"Go ahead," she said.

I opened up the CD box to find a homemade copy of a classical recording. She'd written the name J.S. Bach on the disc, but not the details of the actual works. On the inside cover was scrawled: *Simon, think of me every time you play this. Last night at the concert I was in another world. Thanks forever.*

I turned around. "How long do you need?"

"Not long," she said. "I promise I won't try to escape."

*

I walked down the stairs and sat in her living room, letting it all flood through my mind. I pictured them at the concert together, two people from two different planets, coming together, and each transforming the other: a new creation.

The minutes were ticking when the feeling swept over me.

Something was wrong.

The house seemed suddenly, eerily, silent.

I stood up, shouted, "Beth!"

No response.

I walked to the foot of the staircase and shouted her name again. My voice seemed to echo in the vast silence.

I walked up the stairs, entering the void.

The door to Simon's room was closed. I moved quickly towards it, throwing the door open.

Beth Hilary's lifeless body was swinging over the upturned chair that had taken her fragile weight until she had kicked it away. I took her down, but it was over. She had left the building, gone to find her lost son.

*

Sykes wasn't too hard on me and I repaid the compliment in kind. Maybe there was a hint of deeper understanding and even a hint of mutual respect, though in truth I was too tired and sick to dwell on the possibilities of anything.

At some stage I was taken back to Scolders Rise.

I went upstairs and lay exhausted on my unmade bed. I felt at the package that Beth Hilary had given me though I still hadn't a clue what it might be.

Could I hand my daughter an unchecked present from a dead stranger?

Possibly I could.

I took the cheque from my pocket and looked at it again. I hadn't earned that much in I didn't know how many years. It seemed wrong taking it, and at the same time it didn't seem wrong at all. It would see Roy right, Carl and Angie too – and what was left was going in trust for Josie.

Beth Hilary had cleared out the attic of her life, tearing down the cobwebs, closing the final account. She believed in ghosts and curses … *perhaps*. More than that, she believed in laying them finally to rest.

*

I reached down under the bed, and I came back up with a Chandler and a battered old Poe. But neither of these classics seemed to be in the right frame of mind to communicate with me. Even *The Big Sleep* could only remind me of what I longed to do once my eyes finally closed.

I padded over to the bookcase and chose again. Something I'd read as a child, about a little girl falling down a rabbit hole and having the most ridiculous adventures of all time. Something I could identify with.

Twist

As much as I was enjoying the story, I could feel my eyes getting heavy, and I knew that it was time to turn out the light. I still had the mysterious parcel at the side of my bed, and I gave it one last investigative feel before I switched the light off.

I was still no wiser.

Tomorrow I would ring up Josie's mother and book some arrangements, and Carol, being Carol, would want the details: what I had bought for Josie, what this and what that; and I would bluff the William Twist way, and say that it was a surprise, and that would piss Carol off, and then we would argue. But it would be the truth, at least.

*

I finally switched off the light and lay for a while in the darkness, thinking over everything that had happened; wondering which private rabbit hole I was about to fall down this particular night. Perhaps there would be a parade of delicious women lining up to kiss the hero. Perhaps I would be staring into Todd Cartwright's dead eyes and fearing hell for the last time. Or perhaps it was back east again, to the boy of Simon Hilary's age, or the young constable catching sight of Carol for the first time and feeling so excited that he wanted to scream out a song of joy to the world. Or sitting in Professor Potts' room listening to the riddles of the universe, or in the churchyard with Simon and one day soon no doubt with Beth Hilary ... or else watching a beautiful little girl open her birthday present, as two proud parents asphyxiated on bated breath.

I could no more control my dreams than name the soul. But for the first time in a long time I had optimism on my side, and it had nothing to do with the world of dreaming or the pages of books. Tomorrow was a new day and nothing else in the ragged universe mattered.

Mark L. Fowler

THE END

Printed in Great Britain
by Amazon